# The Secret Ingredient

Also by Laura Schaefer

*The Teashop Girls*

# The Secret Ingredient

## LAURA SCHAEFER

A Paula Wiseman Book

SIMON & SCHUSTER BOOKS FOR YOUNG READERS

New York   London   Toronto   Sydney   New Delhi

*For Aimee Tritt, my favorite foodie*

SIMON & SCHUSTER BOOKS FOR YOUNG READERS
An imprint of Simon & Schuster Children's Publishing Division
1230 Avenue of the Americas, New York, New York 10020

For information about special discounts for bulk purchases, please contact Simon & Schuster Special Sales at 1-866-506-1949 or business@simonandschuster.com.
The Simon & Schuster Speakers Bureau can bring authors to your live event. For more information or to book an event, contact the Simon & Schuster Speakers Bureau at 1-866-248-3049 or visit our website at www.simonspeakers.com.
Also available in a Simon & Schuster Books for Young Readers hardcover edition
Book design by Krista Vossen based on original design by Jessica Handelman
The text for this book is set in Venetian
The illustrations for this book are rendered in pen and ink
Manufactured in the United States of America • 0612 MTN
First Simon & Schuster Books for Young Readers paperback edition June 2012
2 4 6 8 10 9 7 5 3 1
The Library of Congress has cataloged the hardcover edition as follows:
Schaefer, Laura.
The secret ingredient / Laura Schaefer.—1st ed.
p. cm.
"A Paula Wiseman Book."
Sequel to: The Teashop Girls.
Summary: While working at her grandmother's Madison, Wisconsin, teashop, fourteen-year-old Annie hears of a scone cook-off, for which the prize is an all-expenses-paid trip to London for tea, and enlists Genna and Zoe to help her win. Includes proverbs, quotations, and brief stories about tea, as well as recipes.
ISBN 978-1-4424-1959-9 (hc)
[1. Tea—Fiction. 2. Tearooms—Fiction. 3. Grandmothers—Fiction. 4. Best friends—Fiction. 5. Friendship—Fiction. 6. Contests—Fiction. 7. Blogs—Fiction. 8. Madison (Wis.)—Fiction.] I. Title.
PZ7.S33232Sec 2011
[Fic]—dc22
2010032706
ISBN 978-1-4424-1960-5 (pbk)
ISBN 978-1-4424-1968-1 (eBook)

# Acknowledgments

Thank you to my parents, family, and dear friends for their support, suggestions, and well-wishes. It means a lot.

Many thanks to my editor Alexandra Penfold at Simon & Schuster for her enthusiasm, kindness, and awesome baking and photography skills. I am also very grateful to my literary agent Stephen Barbara at Foundry Media for his hard work and encouragement.

Thank you to the teachers, librarians, and teashop owners who have helped me connect with my fabulous readers. Visiting your classrooms, libraries, and shops has been so much fun.

I'd like to acknowledge in particular those who've helped grow my tea knowledge recently by sharing with me their wisdom and, of course, their tea: Giun Kendo, Maleah Moskoff at Chachatea.net, Beth Johnston at TeasEtc.com, and too many others to name, thank you for everything. The tea community is truly full of wonderful people.

Finally, to Brad Carman. You're the best.

## Chapter One

We live in stirring times—tea-stirring times.
—CHRISTOPHER ISHERWOOD

The pumpkin bar with cream cheese frosting from Murphy Farms is the pinnacle of bakery perfection. After a swallow of peach iced tea from my light green water bottle, I grinned at Zoe and took a giant bite.

There were exactly six glorious weeks of summer left to enjoy, and the Madison Farmer's Market on the capitol square was packed with market goers, flowers, veggies, fruit, and signs. We were right in the middle of it all. I gobbled up my bar and tucked into a container of delectable cottage cheese next. After that, a bag of strawberries awaited. I planned to eat every last one of them before my brothers—or worse, Zach Anderson— tracked us down.

"But how do you even know he's down here?" Zoe was asking me. "Wouldn't he rather run through a mud puddle after a Frisbee than look for fresh herbs?"

"Yes," I said. "But he's been bugging me all week at the Leaf, and I accidentally told him I was coming here today. It's like he is incapable of leaving me alone for two hours."

Zoe giggled. "Aw, that's kind of sweet."

"No, it isn't! The worst part is, the customers think he's an actual Leaf employee! So if he says something ridiculous, it makes the shop look bad."

Zoe opened her mouth to reply, but then spotted some truly gorgeous tomatoes. They were just coming into season, and their ruby red color was definitely turning everyone's heads. "Ooh, I'm going to get some of these."

We carefully chose three of the best-looking ones and put them in Zoe's canvas bag. Just then, the crowd cleared up a little and we heard a piercing shriek. A very familiar piercing shriek. "Heeeeeeeeeeeey!"

"Genna!" Zoe and I both yelled. We turned around and there she was, arms outstretched in a show-stopping pose. We raced over to give her a hug and practically knocked over a toddler who tried to get between us.

"Aughhhhh!" we screamed.

"You're home a day early!" I cried. I couldn't believe it. We weren't expecting her until tomorrow.

"I know! I got an earlier flight. I went right to the Steeping Leaf, and Louisa said you were down here," she said from behind ginormous white sunglasses. A few people grumbled as they tried to get around Gen, who had her hands on her hips and a big grin on her face.

"I can't believe you found us so easily," I said.

"I just looked for your hair, Annie!" We giggled. It was so humid, my curly red hair was taking up more space than a small stroller. I saw a college girl trying to sample some cheese shoot us a glare.

"I think we're kind of blocking the way," Zoe said reasonably. We were creating a major bottleneck on the packed sidewalk, so she led us off the square and onto the lush green capitol lawn, where we collapsed into a Teashop Girls pile of happiness.

"You look great, Gen," I said. She did. Her hair had highlights in it, and she wore a magenta shirt dress with a tiny short-sleeved jacket over it.

"Thanks! I missed you guys so much!" We group-hugged again.

"So what did you *do*? How was the food? Did you like the teachers?" I wanted to hear *everything* about camp. Starting with the standing ovations, right down to the mosquito bites.

"Aughhhhhhhh!" Genna exclaimed and bolted up from the grass. Zo and I looked at her, puzzled, until she pulled a new phone out of the pocket of her jacket. She texted madly for a moment and then sunk back down to the grass contentedly. "He misses me. I knew it. I have to get back to New York as soon as *possible*."

"Who?" Zoe asked.

"James. This guy I met. He's a*maz*ing," Genna said. She sounded so happy; like if she was a soda, she'd be bubbling right out of the can. "Your hair is so long!"

Zoe absentmindedly adjusted her headband. "Yeah, I guess it is."

I still didn't have a phone or a boyfriend or any chance of getting either one anytime soon, so I rolled my eyes the teeniest bit. Zoe laughed and took a bite of her pumpkin bar. It was a little smushed from all of the hugging. "Gen. We've finally got you back. You're not running away again," she said in a definite way, and carefully wiped her mouth with a napkin in case there were any specks of frosting left behind. I didn't think to grab a napkin myself . . . oops.

"Now the summer is perfect," I said. Zoe dug through her canvas bag to inspect some fresh herbs she'd bought earlier—basil, parsley, and chives.

"You can have half for your next scone," she said, and suddenly stopped what she was doing to touch my arm. She grinned. "Tell Genna about the contest! I'll go get her a pumpkin bar." Zoe hurried off, gracefully weaving her way through the crowd back to the Murphy Farms stand.

"Well . . . Duchess Teas, one of our big tea suppliers at the Leaf, is running a scone competition for young bakers," I said, clapping my hands together excitedly. "I entered and Louisa is helping me. We have three weeks and, uh, six days left to build a food blog and get followers. The five blogs with the most followers get to go to Chicago in September for a bake-off. We need to invent the best-tasting scone in the world!"

"Oooh, that sounds *fabulous*," Genna said breathily. Her eyes sparkled as much as her glittery nail polish, and I thought about how very, very much I'd missed her all of these weeks. Thank goodness she was back.

"Tell her about the *prize*." Zoe returned, handed Genna a bar, and poked my leg with her flip-flop–clad toe.

"This is the best part for sure." I nodded so hard my hair bounced. "The winners get *four* tickets to London for an all-expenses-paid high tea vacation! Louisa and I already decided, of course, that if we win, we're taking you and Zoe."

"Oh YEAH!" With that, Genna jumped up again, this time pulling Zo and I with her. We all whooped and jumped around until we realized people might be watching us. Giggling, we sat down on the grass and leaned back, enjoying the sunshine on our faces. "So, have you started already? What kind of scone do you think you'll make? What's the blog address? How did you find out about it? Can I help?" Genna's questions tumbled out a mile a minute.

"Um, yes, a delicious one, SteepingLeafScone.com, in *Tea Time* magazine, and absolutely!" I answered.

"We're actually going to buy some ingredients here," Zoe added. "Berries and Hook's cheeses and some fresh herbs."

"Sounds great!" Genna said. I smiled and offered her a heaping spoonful of cottage cheese. She shook her head.

"Your turn. Tell us more about camp," I demanded.

"Oh my God, you guys, it was completely and totally

fabulous," she said. "Like, the best five weeks of my life. Tucked in the woods, memorizing scenes. I got to pretend to be a waterfall. And then a moose. And then a toothbrush. That was kind of hard, actually. But it was wonderful. And I met all of these great, creative people. I know for sure now . . . I don't want to be anything other than an actress. I can even cry on cue. Watch!"

Zoe and I looked at Genna, and within moments, real tears appeared in the corners of her eyes.

"Whoa," Zoe said.

"How did you do that?" I asked.

"Easy. I just think of having to go to *school* again." She grinned, wiped her eyes, and checked her phone before flopping back on the grass. "I wonder if James is looking at the same blue sky," Gen said dreamily. She laid flat on her back, gazing upward.

"I'm sure he is," Zoe said indulgently. "So, what's this James character like?" She laid down too, placing her head close to Genna's.

"He's an aspiring playwright. From New York City. Sixteen, but seems *much* older."

"He does sound amazing," I said kindly. I noticed she hadn't touched the pumpkin bar Zoe had gotten her either. Weird. Mine was gone in four bites.

"Genna, why aren't you eating your bar? Do you feel okay?"

"My what? Oh yeah. I feel fine. I'm just not . . ."

I felt something cold dripping on my arm and realized someone was blocking my sun. I turned around, and there was Zach Anderson, soaking wet and standing over me.

"Zach! Stop dripping on me! You smell like the *lake*." I glared at him and he moved even closer. "Go away!"

"Just did a few laps out to the float at B. B. Clarke," he said, pointing to the beach on Lake Monona about six blocks away.

"Couldn't you *dry off* before you came looking for me?" I asked. Genna and Zoe scooted away from Mr. Algae, but they were giggling.

"Why aren't you back at the Leaf by now?" he asked. "You left Louisa alone all morning?"

"I'm sure she's fine," I said. "She did run the place for thirty years before me, you know."

"But all of that gross powdered tea was coming in today, remember?" Ever since his parents bought our building, Zach was at the Leaf almost as much as me these days. He was *so* annoying, but he did actually help do the dishes sometimes, so I let him hang around.

"Yeah, I'm going to go help her stock when the market's

over. Powdered tea isn't gross. And seriously, stop dripping on me!" I could see Gen's eyebrows move sky-high at the familiar—friendly?—way we were talking to each other.

"No way." Zach shook his head and sprayed me all over again. "Hey, whose pumpkin frosting thing? Can I have it?"

"No . . . it's G—," I started to say.

"Knock yourself out," she finished, and handed it to him. "I don't eat things sprinkled with lake water when I can help it."

"Thumanks," he mumbled, stuffing the entire thing into his mouth.

"You are disgusting," I said.

He swallowed, wiped his mouth with his wet T-shirt, and sat down with us. "So I hope I didn't miss any girl talk," he said. "Teashop Girl talk, I mean. Annie, tell me, how is that new trainer bra fitting?"

I looked at him in horror and crossed my arms in front of my chest. In unison Zoe and I yelled, "ZACH, GO AWAY!" He grinned and walked off to his bike.

"See you back at the Leaf, Annie Green!" he shouted over his shoulder as he sped away.

"You two are so going to get married," Genna said to me with a huge smile on her face. "Now, let's go buy some scone ingredients!"

## <u>To Do Saturday, July 25</u>

- Bake a delicious scone
- Avoid Zach (perhaps invent Annoying Boy Repellent?)
- Get hundreds of blog followers
- Spend as much time with Gen as possible
- Reapply sunscreen constantly
- Buy new clothes for school
- Get haircut

Dear readers,

Welcome to my blog! Thank you SO MUCH for visiting. I'm super excited to participate in the Duchess Tea Company Scone Bake-Off. I hope you'll enjoy following along as I work to create an original, extra-delicious scone. I've been eating these yummy tea treats for forever—with clotted cream and jam, of course—because my grandmother Louisa is the owner of Madison's favorite tea shop, the Steeping Leaf Café on Monroe Street. The shop recently celebrated its thirtieth anniversary in business! Isn't that cool?? (Team Leaf!)

Anyway, I am the newest barista there, but that doesn't mean I'm new to tea. My two best friends and I—Louisa calls us the original Teashop Girls—have loved it practically our whole lives. Recently we all worked together to bring new customers into our very favorite place, to make sure that the Steeping Leaf is around for another thirty years. (At least.) I hope that if you live in Madison or nearby, you'll come by for a nice cuppa. I'd love to read your comments here, but in person's always best, don't you think?

Zoe, Genna, and I started a collection of tea memorabilia when we were little kids and put it all in this ginormous tea handbook. I want to share some of our collection with you here. Between posting scone recipes, I'm going to scan in our best vintage tea ads, pictures, and cards. I hope you love it as much as I do. I'll be sure to keep the handbook in the shop during the scone contest. Please visit me! I'm all ears when it comes to scone recipe suggestions, and I'm there every day this summer. :-) Yay tea, yay scones, yay summer!

Love, Annie

## Chapter Two

We'll see if tea and buns can make the world a better place.
—KENNETH GRAHAME, *THE WIND IN THE WILLOWS*

I arrived at the Leaf two hours later with a canvas bag full to brimming with fresh eggs, goat cheese, basil, chives, and strawberries. The shop was busy, and it was so great to see lots of customers inside and outside, enjoying our patio. Louisa was on what she called her "Bossa nova kick," so we were listening to Stan Getz. She swayed to the Brazilian music behind the counter, measuring out some rooibos for a fresh pot. The light streaming in through the front windows glinted off Louisa's arm of silver bracelets. She wore a pair of plum-colored Capri pants and an ivory tunic decorated with beads. A light summer scarf with silver threads woven through it was draped over her shoulders. I wished for the millionth time that someday I'd dress as well as my grandmother did.

Louisa loved to keep the Steeping Leaf full of fresh flowers in the summer, and the shop smelled amazing. There were roses near the cash register, and a bud vase on each table contained a single daisy. I smiled as I watched people stick their faces in the roses and inhale deeply before making their orders.

"How was the market, sweetness?" She peered at my bag approvingly.

"Perfect," I said. "Genna found us almost right away. She helped me pick out ingredients for our next scone."

"Mmm, what do we have here?" Louisa took a sip of her herbal brew as I unpacked my bag. She handed me a cup as well and I took a small sip. It was pretty warm outside, so I fetched a glass of ice and turned my portion into iced tea.

"I'm not sure if we can put both cheese and strawberries in the same recipe, but I thought it might be interesting to try," I explained.

"Sounds divine," she agreed.

"I got the basil and chives for a second scone recipe." I put everything into the small refrigerator. The teashop was command central for our scone contest preparations.

Both Louisa and I were convinced that all of the well-wishes of our customers would infuse our recipe with extra yumminess. "I saw Zach downtown too."

"How is our very favorite pest?" Louisa asked.

"Fine," I said, blushing a little thinking back to the "trainer bra" incident. There was no way I was mentioning *that* to Louisa. "He said that the matcha arrived. I thought I could help you put it away."

"I did order quite a lot this time. People really seem to have taken a liking to it. Let's put some out for display and tuck the rest away in the cooler," she suggested.

"Sure thing." I went to the storage room to find the shipment and carefully placed some of the rich green powder in an airtight tin. If people wanted to take a look or have a sniff before ordering, they could. Matcha is powdered green tea from Japan. It has a strong flavor, and it's very nutritious. Having one cup of it is like having almost ten cups of regular green tea, since you're actually drinking the tea leaf itself instead of just an infusion. Some people find it a little bitter, but I add a pinch of sweetener to mine and it's just right.

After I finished putting the shipment away, I went around to all of the occupied tables to see if anyone needed new hot water for their tea. I found the Kopinskis out on the patio, with their faces to the sun and their pot of Earl Grey. They wore matching outfits as usual: his-and-hers nylon resort wear in blue.

"Isn't this weather wonderful?" I asked. I cleared a plate and smiled at the couple, two of our best regular customers.

"I can't get enough of it," Mrs. K. agreed. "I'm storing up vitamin D for winter."

"Gah! Don't even mention winter," Mr. Kopinski admonished his wife. "As far as I'm concerned, it doesn't exist." He grinned at both of us. "And how are you, Annie?"

"I'm great. My best friend Genna is back in town and I just went to the farmer's market." Sure, the heat and humidity were making my hair frizz and my forehead shiny, but even that couldn't bug me on such a gorgeous day. I knew my aura was sparkling.

"Ooh, what did you buy this time?" Mrs. Kopinski asked. "Something for your scones?" She knew all about the contest.

"I did. I'm going to bake now, in fact. You should stay put for a sample."

"We wouldn't dream of leaving," Mr. K. said. "Say, is there a newspaper lying around?"

"Yep!" I grabbed the *Wisconsin State Journal* and the *Milwaukee Journal Sentinel* for them from our rack and brought the stack to their table.

"Thank you." The couple expertly split up the paper according to the sections each one wanted to read. Mr. K. took the Travel and Opinion pages; Mrs. K. took Business and Local. I smiled and went back inside the shop. I noticed two customers I'd never seen before sitting by the window at one of our larger tables.

"Hi, I'm Annie. Can I get you fresh water or anything else?" I asked.

"Hello, Annie. Some water would be great," the young man said. His hair was twisted up into short dreadlocks, and he wore small wire-rim glasses. "I'm Oliver, and this is my wife, Theresa. We just moved to the neighborhood."

"Your shop is so nice," Theresa said. She had very long hair and a kind smile. I grinned as we shook hands.

"Thank you! My grandmother has run it for a *long* time. We just had our thirtieth-anniversary party two months ago," I explained as I refilled their pot. "Where are you from?"

"Atlanta. We moved because Oliver got a new job. I was worried we wouldn't be able to find good tea here, but I see now there won't be any trouble," Theresa said, satisfied. I noticed they were drinking our best jasmine oolong.

"If you have any special variety in mind that you don't see on our shelves, just let myself or Louisa know. We're always happy to order whatever our neighbors like."

"Thank you," Oliver said. "I'm sure we'll be back."

"Wonderful! Nice to meet you both," I added.

Even though I knew that the Leaf was out of the woods now that our rent was lower, I still made an extra effort with each and every customer. I wanted them to be so pleased with their tea, food, and service that they couldn't help but tell their friends about us. I knew Louisa did the same thing. But the exciting thing was I could tell she was more willing to try new things now, like take a risk on a tea we hadn't sold before. The whole place felt fresher.

Since all the customers were taken care of, I pulled a large earthenware bowl out from behind the counter— it was handmade pottery, a gift from one of the Leaf's old customers—and began thinking about the scones I wanted to bake. I began with a simple base of flour, baking powder, pinch of salt, butter, buttermilk, and egg. Louisa had shown me the week before how to mix the dry ingredients together first, then to add the wet ones. Next, I carefully worked the dough together. Thank goodness I did it right this time. I wasn't exactly a natural when it came to scones, and I had ruined a batch last week by adding the milk too soon. Scones are harder to make than cookies. But more fun to eat!

"Very nice," Louisa said, peering over my shoulder. "What sort of specialness will you add to this one, dearheart?"

"Do you think the strawberries will work with the goat cheese?" I was still learning a lot about what flavors went together. Since the contest was for young bakers, it was up to me to come up with the recipe, but Louisa chimed in with advice when I wanted her to.

"Hmm. I love *chevre*," she said. Louisa used the French word for goat cheese, which I couldn't even say. "But it's such a soft variety that I'm worried it might melt during baking. Why don't we grate some Parmesan instead for the dough and save the goat cheese for spreading on our biscuits?"

"Good idea," I said. I added the berries to the dough and found a wedge of Parmesan in the fridge. After grating a little under a cup, I added that, too. Finally, I added "the secret ingredient" to the recipe. Louisa winked as she watched me do it. Then I formed the dough into a round and used my mini scone cutter to make little shapes. I placed them on a greased baking sheet and brushed the top of each one with milk. Each time I tried a new recipe, I only did one pan in case they didn't turn out. These looked promising, though. I placed them in the oven at 400 degrees. Within ten minutes the shop was filled with the delicious smell of melty Parmesan goodness.

"Annie, this contest is great for business," Louisa whispered conspiratorially. "Look!"

I looked around the shop as one after another, every customer's head popped up. It was almost as if you could see the waft of scone aroma float under their noses and lift up their chins. I giggled. After five more minutes I pulled the creations out of our oven to cool and announced that everyone would get one to try—on the house. People actually applauded!

"I can't wait to try them, dearest," Louisa said.

"Me either!"

As the scones cooled, I wandered back to the office and booted up Louisa's ancient desktop computer. We only had a dial-up connection at the Steeping Leaf, but I wanted to do a quick blog entry about my recipe. I wish I'd thought of doing a website for the shop earlier, in fact. It was good business for the Leaf. After the customers had a chance to try them, I'd go back and add their impressions and suggestions.

When I was able to finally bring up the blog page, I looked with satisfaction at the two recipes I'd already posted: one for maple nut scones and the chocolate chip scone one I had posted that morning. I already had seven followers. I eagerly checked for new comments.

**Miss Cuppycake:** These chocolate chip scones look so good I could eat four and ask for more. Your glaze recipe for maple nut scones sounds heavenly! Nice job.

July 25 9:55 a.m.

Everyone was very complimentary. I scrolled down, smiling.

**ElizaJ3000:** Maple nut scones are my favorite kind of scone. I wish I lived in Madison so I could come to the Leaf and try yours. ☺

July 25 10:57 a.m.

Aw, sweet!

My heart stopped when I read the latest comment.

**SweetCakes:** These are very UNORIGINAL. You don't have a prayer in September, Steeping Leaf!!

July 25 11:02 a.m.

What? Who on earth was SweetCakes? And why did she have it out for me?

**Chocolate Chip Scones**

Now, for all our junior Teashop Girls club members at home, remember to ask your parents before you start the recipe below, or any others. Scones and other teashop treats aren't super easy to make, and you might need a grown-up's help or supervision. Have fun! <3 Annie

**Ingredients**

⅔ cup sugar

2 cups flour

1 tablespoon baking powder

1 cup mini dark chocolate chips

¼ teaspoon salt

3 tablespoons cold butter

1 egg

½ cup buttermilk

½ tablespoon vanilla

½ teaspoon secret ingredient

¼ cup whole milk

Preheat your oven to 400 degrees Fahrenheit. Mix sugar, flour, baking powder, mini dark chocolate chips, and salt. Cut in cold butter. In a separate bowl whisk the egg, vanilla, and the buttermilk. Slowly add the wet mix to the dry mix and stir to combine until even. Add the secret ingredient. Knead the dough together a few times until the dough is one solid ball. Roll out the dough into a circle, about an inch thick or less. Use cookie cutter to cut out small circles. Place scone circles on a greased cookie tray. Brush with milk. Bake for 15 to 17 minutes until golden brown. Makes 12 scones. Serve warm!

July 25  8:03 a.m.

## Chapter Three

Tea was such a comfort.
—EDNA ST. VINCENT MILLAY

Louisa could tell something was wrong the moment she looked at my face. I came back out of the office before I'd even posted my third recipe. The scones were almost ready to taste, and she was using a small spatula to place them on a tiered plate to hand out around the shop. There was a small digital camera at her side. We took pictures of all of our efforts. Even if they didn't end up tasting good, they sure *looked* great!

"Annie, love, what's the matter?"

"Nothing really," I said, and tried to smile again. "It's just that someone left a kind of rude comment on our blog. I'm sure they didn't mean anything by it," I added quickly. I picked up the camera and took a photo of the little scones on their pretty tiers.

"I don't understand the Internet," Louisa said. "It seems like people can say whatever they want on there and no one shames them for forgetting their manners."

"You've got that right," I said. "It's okay. Let's try these!" Ever since the contest had kicked off a few days ago, I'd been obsessively checking the leader board to see who had the most blog followers. The rule was that every entrant had to start a brand-new food blog; you couldn't enter if you already ran a popular one. But I wondered what tricks some of the others were using, because the Steeping Leaf was in dismal thirty-second place, with just a handful of followers. The kids at the top already had a few hundred! They were probably high school students with about a million Facebook friends. If only my mom wasn't so strict about how much time I spent on the computer. Sigh. The people I had to beat in order to get to London probably already had smart cell phones and I didn't even have a dumb one.

I placed one of my mini scones on a napkin, pulled it apart a little, and blew on it. The Parmesan had melted into the nooks and crannies of the creamy dough. The bright red strawberries made them look very festive. I took a bite.

"Oh, yum," I said. Louisa took a bite as well.

"Delicious, Annie!" Louisa carefully set one of them aside. I bet it was for Mr. Arun. They were still having, as she called it, a dalliance. My former principal had come into the Leaf exactly once since summer started. But my barista cheer couldn't hide how awkward I felt with him there being lovey-dovey with my grandmother. Fortunately for me, after that they conducted their rendezvous in other locales. "Do you think this is the one?"

"It's good, but I don't know if it's the *one*. Let's see what the customers think." I handed out each scone to the eager Steeping Leaf crowd. Many of them had already heard about my contest.

I gave the Kopinskis two scones on the patio and another one to two ladies who were walking by but stopped in their tracks when they saw me handing out samples.

"It's for a baking contest I entered," I said a bit shyly. "If you like it, please follow me on SteepingLeafScone. com so I can be a finalist."

"Thanks! We will," they said, tasting my latest scone.

"Mmm. That was great," said one wearing a big sun hat.

I smiled and turned to go back inside, but then the sun-hatted lady asked, "What was that address again?" Both of the women had their phones out.

"SteepingLeafScone.com." I grinned. Two more followers! Just like that.

"Annie, this might be your best one yet," Mr. Kopinski said. He patted his belly happily. "I hope you and your grandmother add it to the permanent menu." Mrs. K. nodded in agreement and neatly wiped her mouth with a napkin.

"It goes so well with the Earl Grey," she said.

"Wow, I never thought about that, but maybe we will. Thanks!" It seemed the scone was a hit.

Next, I took two samples over to Oliver and Theresa.

"I love how the saltiness of the Parmesan mixed with the sweetness of the berries," Theresa said, dabbing her mouth with a napkin. "It reminds me of something my mother used to make when I was little. Nice work!"

"Thanks!" After everyone was finished, I returned to the office to do my post. Even though I tried not to think about the mean commenter, I couldn't help but congratulate myself on the latest scone's originality. I had never before seen this particular type of scone anywhere.

*Take that, SweetCakes!*

The whole point of the blogs was to collaborate and get ideas from other bakers, not zing them. I reread my post three times, hesitating to hit the "Publish Post" button. I felt a bit jittery, wondering if anyone would comment on my new scone. Finally, I did it. I let out a breath and refreshed the page a few times after the post was up, hoping for an instant comment. None appeared, of course, so I turned off the computer and went back out into the shop.

I placed the two remaining scones in a little box for Zoe and Genna. Zo would be in any minute for hers, and Genna and I planned to spend the next day together, so I'd give it to her in the morning. Since Genna had missed my birthday, she was treating me to my first-ever pedicure at the Samadhi Spa. My mom said yes when I asked her, which was a minor miracle. She, of course, went off about how *she* had never had a professional pedicure, so I made a mental note to tell Dad he should get her a gift certificate for *her* birthday.

It would just be me and Gen. I was really looking forward to it. It would give me a chance to hear more about mysterious theater camp and the amazing James.

I cleaned up the Leaf's cooking area and washed the bowl and baking sheet. The afternoon tea hour was coming to an end and the shop quieted down. The sun was still high and people wanted to sit in their air-conditioning, which we did not have in the shop. I was thinking about heading home to read some cookbooks or a novel in front of a fan, when I heard the chimes on the door sound their distinctive trill. Zoe popped in just then with a plate.

"I made a quiche!" she announced.

Louisa laughed. "The Teashop Girls certainly do like turning on the oven during the hottest days of the year."

"Ooh, let's see," I said. "What's in it?"

"The vegetables are all organic and from my plot in the community garden, and I used fresh eggs from free-range chickens. Best of all . . . ," she said, unwrapping the foil, "it's still warm."

"It looks lovely, dear," Louisa said as she admired Zoe's quiche.

Free-range chickens are chickens that never live in cages, Zoe had explained to me earlier in the summer. They get to run around a coop outside. It was really important to Zo to get eggs from this kind of farm, now that she'd learned more about it from her fellow community gardeners. I could see the quiche had bright red tomatoes and green flecks of herbs. Zoe had been volunteering her time at the garden near our neighborhood. She'd been learning lots of interesting things about organic food. We'd always adored coming to the weekly farmer's market on the capitol square, but now Zo had given me a new reason to love it even more. She said food grown nearby is good for the environment. And often tastier, since it can be harvested at the peak of ripeness.

"Yum. Let me grab some forks," Louisa said as we tucked in.

"I've been eating all day long!" I exclaimed. "It's really terrific, Zoe. I didn't know you were such a good cook."

"It was actually mostly my stepdad. I just got all the veggies. Aren't the tomatoes great?"

They were. Zoe's quiche was full of those cute small bright red ones. I think they're called grape tomatoes. They kind of exploded when you bit into them. Zoe said they had just ripened.

"They are incredible, dear," Louisa said. "Do you have any left over? Annie might want them for a future scone."

"Definitely! We could even sun-dry them first," Zoe suggested. "It's totally hot enough."

"Would you like any tea?" I offered.

"Always," she said.

## Parmesan Berry Scones

This scone was inspired by my trip to the Madison Farmer's Market this morning. I wanted to combine our state's amazing cheese (On Wisconsin!) with the bright and delicious berries now in season.

### Ingredients

2 cups all-purpose flour

1 tablespoon baking powder

½ cup sugar

½ teaspoon salt

3 tablespoons cold butter

1 egg

⅔ cup buttermilk

1 cup grated Parmesan cheese

1 cup strawberries

½ teaspoon secret ingredient

¼ cup whole milk

Preheat the oven to 400 degrees Fahrenheit. Mix the dry ingredients together first, then cut in the butter. Stir in one beaten egg and add cheese and berries. Add the secret ingredient. Slowly add the buttermilk to form a thick dough. You may need slightly more than ⅔ cup. Knead the dough on a board, roll to a 1-inch thickness, and cut the dough into 2-inch triangles or rounds. Place each scone on a greased cookie sheet and brush the tops with milk. Bake for 12 to 15 minutes until golden brown. Let cool for a few minutes; serve warm. Makes about 12 scones.

**Customer comments about the finished scones:**

"That was great!" "Your best one yet!"

July 25  3:30 p.m.

## Chapter Four

The tea was so delicious that it was not necessary to pretend
it was anything but tea.
—FRANCES HODGSON BURNETT

**SCONE CONTEST LEADER BOARD**

1. Miss Cuppycake.........345 followers
2. Master Baker............301 followers
3. HaileyCakes.............290 followers
4. PastrySwagger..........207 followers
5. Wis-scone-sin...........198 followers
6. SweetCakes.............196 followers

The next morning I was so disheartened to see SweetCakes
near the top of the board. How could a mean person do
so well? I quickly visited her blog. It looked like it had
been professionally designed. Instead of using a standard

template like SteepingLeafScone.com had, SweetCakes.com was unique and full of amazing photos. She had just put up a recipe for White Chocolate Macadamia Nut Scones, and she already had a ton of comments.

**SweetCakesLuver:** YUM.

July 26 9:52 a.m.

**REALFoodie:** I tried this recipe. It is incredible

July 26 9:53 a.m.

**SweetTooth89:** I love your recipes, what kind of flour do you use?

July 26 9:54 a.m.

**BakeAndShake:** LOVE LOVE LOVE NOM NOM NOM

July 26 9:55 a.m.

**SweetCakes:** @SweetTooth89: I use Gold Medal, of course ;-)

July 26 9:56 a.m.

**SweetCakesLuver:** LOL Of course. Because that is what you deserve!!!!!!!!!

July 26 9:57 a.m.

**KiKiCakester:** Do you deliver?

July 26 9:58 a.m.

I scanned the rest of the leader board until I saw what I was looking for:

**29. SteepingLeafScone......15 followers**

I had a *lot* of work to do.


Genna knocked on our front door twenty minutes before our spa appointment. Of course, Luke and Billy had to beat me to it. The boys threw open the door.

"ANNNNNIEEEEE," Billy screeched. "It's GENNNNNNNA!"

Next, Luke ran almost right into her and stuck out his tongue, to reveal it was green from the Popsicle he'd been eating. They pounce on pretty much anyone who comes to the door. My dad says it's a good security system, because most burglars have a natural fear of boys holding skateboards, cleats, and Popsicles melting down their arms. Molly added to the commotion with a few cheerful barks, and Truman watched from his usual perch at the front window. My parents were in the backyard putting new stone edging around the shrubs. It was easily ninety degrees outside, so I was very relieved not to be dragged into it.

From the top of the stairs I could hear Genna using her best voice of authority with my little brothers. "Billy,

Luke, this is a new shirt. If you get any Popsicle juice on me, I *will* make you sorry you were born."

"Hey, Gen! Luke! Billy! Stop!" I grabbed my knapsack and edged out past my brothers.

"Hi, Annie. Ooh, cute sandals, are those new?"

"They're Beth's. She said I could borrow them because my old flip-flops might scare the fancy spa ladies." I grinned. Genna giggled. "Sorry about my brothers," I said as I shut the door firmly behind me. "My dad said he'd take them to the pool, but the yard work is taking longer than he thought it would. They're bouncing off the walls."

"Ha-ha, I don't mind," Genna said. "I like your brothers."

"I guess they're okay when they aren't getting something sticky and purple on me," I said. "But then again, I can't think of a time when they're not."

"So, what color are you gonna pick for your toes?" Genna asked. "I'm thinking about Tantalizing Tangerine."

"That sounds cool. I don't know, I guess I'll see what looks good." My toes were usually just their natural color, so I supposed any color of polish would look cute. "I'm so glad you are back!"

"Me too. Well, sort of." Gen looked wistful. "It's weird. It's like now that I've gone away, I'll always miss something. When I'm here, I miss there. I wish James could come and live in Madison."

"Yeah." I could imagine how Genna was feeling, but not exactly. I'd never been away from home, really, not even for camp. I should probably try it sometime. "So, is he your, you know, boyfriend?"

"Yes. Well, um, I'm not really sure. It seemed like he was when I was there, but now I don't know. We didn't really talk about it. I didn't want to say anything weird because he's, like, a year older than us and lives in *the city*."

"What does living in 'the city' have to do with it?" Was she talking about New York? Wasn't Madison a city?

"I don't know. Things are different there." Genna looked pained. I decided to change the subject, because I didn't really understand what she meant and I didn't want her to be upset during our special spa day.

"So the Leaf was totally full yesterday," I said cheerfully.

"Awesome!" Gen seemed to snap out of it and smiled genuinely. "We can stop by after our toes are done to show Louisa."

"For sure. Oh! That reminds me. I brought you a scone from the batch we made yesterday. Parmesan berry." I reached into my bag for the little pastry box and handed it to Genna. She didn't take it, though.

"What's in it?"

"Oh, the usual stuff, plus the cheese and berries. Totally

yum," I answered. She took it and put it into her bag.

"Cool. I'll have it later."

We walked to Monroe Street and headed toward the university. It was *so* hot. I was glad I'd chosen to wear my loose cotton sundress. I hoped it was appropriate spa garb. Before school started, I planned to do a little clothes shopping with Genna and Zoe to make sure I made a good impression when high school began. Once Beth moved out, I wouldn't be able to dip into her closet when I wanted to look extra nice. And I *definitely* wanted to look extra nice for ninth grade. More grown-up. Just as long as Genna didn't try to get me to wear leggings or berets. Ugh.

When we arrived, the spa was very quiet, just like I remembered it. I loved the faint smell of eucalyptus in the air—it made it seem like we were in the tropics or something. The nice receptionist lady asked if we wanted any tea—supplied by the Steeping Leaf, of course! Both Genna and I nodded happily. The tea was our organic green blended with peppermint leaves. It was served hot in gorgeous celadon teacups. I inhaled its delicious smell and already felt totally pampered.

"Seriously, Gen. This is the best. I missed you so much, and being here reminds me of all the great stuff we did to save the Leaf." Genna and Zoe had helped me all spring to get new customers into my grandmother's shop. We chalked advertisements around the neighborhood and handed out samples at school and got the spa to offer our tea.

"Me too! Ooh, look, the newest magazines." Genna eagerly grabbed a pile of super glossy and colorful celebrity weeklies and tossed me one. I grinned. I wondered if I'd ever wear high heels as complicated as the ones the actresses wore. Probably not, if I wanted to make it through college with unbroken ankles. "Oh my gosh!" Gen yelled. She held one magazine very close to her face.

"What?" I looked up immediately, concerned.

"It's Cecily Stevens," she said, pointing to a picture of a young girl I didn't recognize.

"Huh. She's really skinny," I observed.

"I knooow," Genna said, moaning miserably. "And James, like, *knows* her. They went to elementary school together. Now she's on *TV*."

My eyes widened. To me, the girls in the magazines might as well have been from a different planet for all that we had in common. But it seemed like for Genna, they were much, much closer.

"You are *so* much prettier, Gen. And it sounds like the Amazing James knows that," I said comfortingly. "Besides, look what she's holding in that picture. Coffee.

Maybe it'll stain her teeth." It felt kind of mean saying that since I had no idea who she was, but Genna grinned.

"I guess. But still, I'm totally eating only egg whites and vegetables until Christmas. I mean it."

I frowned. It all made sense now, why Genna hadn't eaten her pumpkin bar at the market or her scone just now.

"But Gen, why? You're already perfect. That seems really . . . severe."

"I'm not like you. I can't eat a bunch of cupcakes and still wear kids' sizes. And I don't play tennis three hours a day like Zoe. I have to be careful," she said firmly.

The kids' sizes comment stung. Genna wasn't trying to be mean, but I still felt uncomfortable. Sure, she had looked more, um, womanly than me for the last year or two, but since when was *that* a bad thing? I was so confused.

"Annie and Genna? We're ready for you!" the receptionist sang. I set the glossy magazine down gratefully and stood up. I smiled at Gen and vowed to forget about skinny alien starlets for the afternoon. I hoped she would too.

# SteepingLeafScone.com

Dear readers,

I love drinking tea, but did you know it's good for other things as well? Like beauty! I'm taking a break from baking today to go to the spa with one of my BFFs. You can treat yourself to some at-home spa time with tea!

## Tea Toner

Steep a generous portion of green tea in ½ cup of hot water for 4 minutes. Mix together with ½ cup of aloe gel (look for soothing aloe gel near the sunscreen at your drugstore or grocery store). Apply this mixture to your face in the morning or at night. It's great for sensitive skin!

## Herbal Tea Facial

Steep a tablespoon of peppermint tea in a large teapot. After 2 to 3 minutes of steeping, pour the tea into a bowl. Hold your face directly over the bowl, and place a towel over your head and the bowl. You can soak up the steam for as long as you feel like it. Your pores will clear out, and the peppermint aromatherapy will wake you right up!

xoxo,
Annie

July 26  9:12 a.m.

## Chapter Five

Come oh come ye tea-thirsty restless ones—the kettle boils,
bubbles and sings, musically.
—RABINDRANATH TAGORE

G ross! What *is* that?" Zach had arrived at
the Leaf a moment earlier, propped his bike
almost right against an occupied patio table,
and marched up to the counter, where I was mixing up a
new batch of scones.

"Zach, move your bike. Those people aren't valets," I
said. "They're our *customers.*"

He sighed massively and went back outside. Louisa handed
me a half cup of dried tomatoes for the recipe and winked
at me. "Can we ban him from the shop?" I asked her. Even
though it was Monday, typically our slowest day of the week,
I didn't want Zach to disturb the peaceful Steeping Leaf aura.

"I don't think so, dear. We'll just make him grate some cheese and he'll settle down."

"That's what my mom is always trying to do with Billy and Luke, and they usually just mess up whatever she's trying to make," I replied. Louisa chuckled.

Zach came back in, plopped himself heavily on a counter stool, and poked his finger into my scone dough.

"ZACH! Cut it out! You'll contaminate my recipe!" I shouted, and grabbed the bowl away protectively. Louisa made a noise that sounded suspiciously like laughter.

"What sort of crime against nature are you making this time?" he asked. Zach knew about the contest and he knew how important it was to me, but he insisted on being a pain about it. "And don't worry, my hands are clean. All I've done all day is play disc golf."

"Great. I'm sure that is really sanitary," I said sarcastically. "It's going to be scones with dried grape tomatoes, bacon, and sharp cheddar. You can have one when they're done."

"No way. I don't eat girl food."

"Scones aren't girl food!" I said.

"Um, yes, they are. The *girliest*."

Louisa could see that I was getting mad, so she handed Zach a warm soapy dish towel. "Here, young man, wash your hands. You can help the lovely Annie grate some cheese."

Zach was awful, but he couldn't resist my grandmother.

He took the rag, made a face at me, and dutifully washed and dried his hands. I was surprised when he actually took the block of cheese and did a good job grating it. Louisa said something about getting a fresh bulb of garlic from the garden and disappeared out the back door.

"Here you go, *lovely* Annie." He handed me the cheese board with a neat pile.

"Why, thank you, *terrible* Zach," I said. I added the cheese to my dough and kneaded it in with my hands.

"That is so disgusting," he said. My dough was speckled with red tomatoes, orange cheese, and crispy bacon pieces. "It looks like upchuck. You are not going to win, you know."

I narrowed my eyes at him. Then I gave him a sympathetic smile. "Oh *Zach*, it's okay. I know you are nervous about living your sad existence without me when I go to London for two weeks, but I'm sure you'll survive, somehow. Maybe we can take an ad out in the newspaper and find you some friends."

"How *sweet* of you, lovely Annie," he said, and stuck his finger in the dough again and fished out a piece of bacon. At least they were slightly cleaner now. I smiled, genuinely, because I noticed he didn't sound that sarcastic when he called me "lovely" this time. Then another thought occurred to me. Who would run the Leaf when we *did* win first prize?

"Zach, I just thought of something."

"Your hair looks like you stole it from Carrot Top?"

"*No.*"

"You actually didn't graduate eighth grade and you'll have to repeat middle school as a tragic, too-old freak?"

"Stop it. No, I just realized that when we do win the prize and take our trip, there is no one to run the shop. Too bad Jonathan had to take that job waiting tables downtown."

"Aw, Annie G. misses her One True Love." Zach snickered.

"Not really." I didn't even bother to deny I had a crush on my former fellow barista. It seemed like a long time ago. "But we are going to have to train someone. Listen, do you think you know how much tea goes into a pot? You're here all the time anyway."

"Forget it. I'm not going to get a job, ever. See, there's this thing called a 'trust fund.' Oh wait, you're one of the unwashed masses. You wouldn't understand."

"Have I mentioned lately that I'd rather clean the patio with a toothbrush than talk to you?" I asked.

"I'm pretty sure you said something like that Saturday," he said, unconcerned.

"Good."

I added the "secret ingredient," finished shaping the dough into a flat patty, and cut it into small triangles.

Then I put them on the greased cookie sheet, took a photo, and popped the scones into the oven.

When Louisa returned to the counter, I headed back to the office to start a new blog entry. Zach, of course, followed me.

I sat down at the computer, planning to ignore him, and he started poking around the storage shelves.

"What are you doing?" I finally asked.

"I noticed the oolong is getting low up front."

"Oh." I shook my head, surprised he was deciding to be helpful, and turned back to the computer to flip it on. I was thinking about the measurements I had used for the new scone so I could record them on the blog when I heard Zach drop something.

"Oops," he said.

"Zach! Be careful!" I leaped up out of my chair and went to see what he'd managed to destroy.

"It's just one of the tea shipments, nothing broke," he said, sounding contrite. I picked up the spilled box and carefully put the packages it contained back on the highest shelf. Unfortunately, as I reached above me, I lost my balance a bit. *Not again*, I thought, as I fell over and landed ungracefully on my butt. The packages plopped down all around me, but miraculously none of them opened up. *That* was close.

Zach stood there looking at me sprawled out on the

floor. I stared back at him and neither one of us said anything. There was something strange about his expression. He looked confused. Was he worried I was hurt? It wasn't like an ambulance would be necessary; I doubted I even had a bruise. I groaned and made a move to get up; Zach reached down to give me a hand. I took it and he pulled me up . . . and sort of *toward* him.

The next thing that happened absolutely shocked me.

Zach Anderson *kissed* me.

I was so surprised I forgot to even close my eyes. His lips were soft, and he smelled surprisingly good up close. In an instant it was over, and he was stumbling out of the storage room. I touched my lips and blinked.

When my heart slowed back down to its normal speed and I went back out into the shop, he was gone.

### Annie's Delicious Bacon Scones

I invented these scones after my family ate at this pub called Mickey's on the near east side of Madison. They have the "World's Greatest Sandwich" there, and it is full of bacon. It really is the world's greatest. ☺

### Ingredients

2 cups all-purpose flour

1 tablespoon baking powder

2 tablespoons sugar

½ teaspoon salt

3 tablespoons cold butter

2 eggs

¾ cup grated sharp cheddar cheese

½ cup sun-dried tomatoes, diced

½ cup crumbled crispy bacon

¾ cup buttermilk

½ teaspoon secret ingredient

1 tablespoon milk

Preheat the oven to 400 degrees Fahrenheit. Mix the dry ingredients together first, then cut in the butter. Add the secret ingredient. In a small bowl beat one egg. Stir in the beaten egg and add cheese, tomatoes, and bacon. Slowly add the buttermilk to form a thick dough. You may need slightly more than ¾ cup. Knead the dough on a board, roll to a 1-inch thickness, and cut the dough into 2-inch triangles. Place each triangle on a greased cookie sheet, beat the remaining egg with milk, and brush the tops with the egg wash. Bake for about 12 to 15 minutes until golden brown; serve warm. Makes 12 scones.

July 27  3:12 p.m.

## Chapter Six

To kiss is like drinking tea from a tea-strainer—
you always want more.
—OLD CHINESE SAYING

This is an emergency meeting of the Teashop Girls. I now call us to order. On the docket is a highly fascinating and romantic Steeping Leaf storage-room event involving Zach Anderson," Genna announced loudly.

"Genna!" I protested. Jeez, people could probably hear her all the way down on State Street.

Genna and Zoe and I were at a table on the Leaf patio later that evening. We had a pot of jasmine tea in front of us and three scones, which had indeed turned out fabulously. Fortunately Louisa had rescued them from the oven at the exact right moment. I'd been wandering around all afternoon like someone who'd been hypnotized, and I'd forgotten about them. Louisa asked me if I was coming down with the flu, and I said the hot weather had slowed down my brain. I don't think she bought it, but she didn't say anything.

"Shhhhhh!" I said. "You don't have to announce my first kiss to the entire town."

"Why not? It's totally exciting," she said. "Didn't I *say* you guys were going to get married? I love being right. And come on, you've got to admit Z. is really cute. You know, when he isn't *talking*."

I looked at her and scrunched up my nose.

"Um, there is a big difference between stumbling into someone's face and marrying them," Zoe pointed out reasonably. "It *is* pretty exciting, though, Annie," she added with a giggle. Her white clothes were perfect, as always. I wondered if her mom was doing extra laundry now that Zoe had taken up gardening. Even though my friend was now up close and personal with dirt, there was never a speck of it on her.

"I don't know. It's *Zach*. I didn't really think . . ." I trailed off. I didn't know what to think. I couldn't pretend that my stomach didn't have butterflies in it. Good butterflies. But he was *so obnoxious*. I never thought I would want Zach Anderson to kiss me.

Let alone want him to kiss me again.

"Tell me everything again. Every detail," Genna demanded.

"I fell over and he pulled me off the floor. I ended up sort of right in front of him, and it just *happened*," I said. "It was really quick. But nice."

"When James kissed me, it wasn't really quick," Genna said, dreamily. "I never wanted it to end. Oh Annie, I'm so jealous. You're so lucky Zach lives here. You can start high school with a real boyfriend!"

"I . . . guess," I said. I couldn't even imagine what I'd say to him when I saw him again. Just thinking about it made my face turn pink. I could feel the heat in my cheeks as we spoke.

"Now we just have to find a cute boy for you, Zo," Genna decided.

"I'm good, thanks," Zoe said, and crossed her eyes. "These scones are phenomenal, Annie. What's in them?"

"Some of those tomatoes you gave me, Hook's cheddar, crispy bacon, flour, buttermilk . . . and the secret ingredient, of course." I leaned in and whispered, "Tea leaves!"

"Perfect. Try it, Gen," Zoe prodded.

Genna looked uncomfortable and took a tiny bite. I frowned. I'd momentarily forgotten about her plan to eat nothing but egg whites and celery. "Very good," she said enthusiastically.

"You have to eat more than that!" Zoe protested.

"I can't," Genna said. "I'm on a strict diet."

"You are? Is something wrong? Are you sick?" Zoe immediately looked very concerned. She knew all about my sister, Beth, and her celiac disease. Food allergies could be serious business.

"No, no, nothing like that. I'm just staying away from fat and sugar. It's no big deal."

"Oh," Zoe said. "So you can't eat Annie's scones?"

"I can, but only a taste. This really is delicious, Annie. I know you'll win."

"Thanks," I said. I thought about how Zoe had brought tomatoes to the Leaf for me and how I'd hoped the contest would be sort of a group effort. I wanted Genna to do more than take a tiny taste each time I made a new recipe, but what could I say? She was so determined to look like Cecily, with her ribbony arms. Zoe and I exchanged concerned looks.

"Does your mom know about this diet?" Zoe asked.

"Oh yeah. She's on it too," Genna said breezily. "We got a new juicer." So that explained why Mrs. Matthews always looked sort of pinched. She was hungry. I thought about how *my* mom looked. A bit tired, I guess, but also amused . . . and content. My family always joked around during dinner and ate massive quantities of lasagna or stir-fry or baked chicken with rosemary and mashed potatoes. The thought of trading that in for some egg whites and skinny arms made me sad.

"Anyway, when are you going to see Zach again?" Genna asked. "You want to borrow some of my makeup?"

"I have no idea," I answered. "He's always just kind of popping up. Maybe he'll come to the shop tomorrow . . . I'm working all day."

"Nice."

"I'm not sure how to put on the eye stuff, but I do like your lip gloss a lot," I added warmly.

"Really? Thanks! It's called Peach Sparkles. I have two; you can totally take this one." She reached into her bag and handed it to me.

"Thanks, Gen."

"So, what are you all eating on this diet? You know, the human body needs at least *some* fat." Zoe was determined not to let it go. I shifted in my chair uneasily.

"I promise I'm eating healthfully," Genna said emphatically. "Lots of veggies. And I'm thinking of doing one of those cleanse things and having juice for a few days."

"WHAT? Genna, that is not a good idea. Your body is still growing, and . . . and . . ." Zoe was really upset. She had a point.

"It's fine. Don't wig out," Genna said defensively. "Jeez."

"I'm not wigging out. I'm worried about you," Zoe replied. "What have you eaten today?"

"Stop being the food police. It's none of your business. Annie, tell her to drop it."

"Um . . ." I looked back and forth between my two best friends and didn't say anything.

"Genna, let Louisa make you a turkey sandwich with some yogurt for dinner. I'll go ask her." Zoe stood up and Genna did too.

"Forget it. I'm going to eat what I want to eat. I'm leaving." Genna glared at Zoe and stomped out of the patio. Zoe sat down heavily, took a huge bite of her scone, and chewed angrily. I'd never seen her get so upset at Genna before. I didn't know what to say.

## To Do: Tuesday, July 28

- Get Genna to eat more than a bite of something.
- Invent best scone recipe in the history of scone recipes.
- Get one thousand blog followers.
- Try kissing again. Maybe.
- Calm down. For real.

Dear readers,

Remember when I said I'd share some of the vintage ads I've collected in the Teashop Girls Handbook? Here is one of my favorites. It's from when Louisa was a little girl.

Have you ever tried Teaberry gum? It's delicious! This gum has been around practically forever (okay, since 1900, close enough). It's made with flavors from the Eastern Teaberry bush, which is an evergreen shrub that produces an oil similar in taste to wintergreen. Even though there isn't technically any actual tea in Teaberry gum, I still heart it. ☺ It's the perfect gum to have after high tea.

<3 Annie

July 27  7:13 p.m.

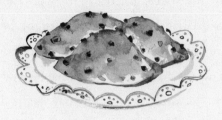

## Chapter Seven

Make tea, not war.
—Monty Python

The next day, I woke up earlier than I usually do. I could hear the reassuring sound of a cardinal chirping outside of my window, but it was impossible to lie there and enjoy it like I normally could. Yes, I was worried about Genna and Zoe's spat, but more than that I was confused about what had happened between Zach and me. When I thought about it, I couldn't help but smile, like I held a very precious secret inside of me. I practically wanted to giggle. All this time, Zach *liked* me. It was incredible. But also so very strange. I couldn't imagine how I would talk to him now. Would he still tease me and say mean things? How would I feel if he did?

I just knew I wanted to see him as soon as possible to find out what would happen next.

I threw off my sheet, got ready for work, and grabbed the day's to-do list I had made the night before. The shop didn't open for another half hour, but I could always help Louisa water her plants and maybe start another blog post. It was sure to be a hot day again. I put on a light cotton blouse and jean skirt and grabbed my Leaf apron. My hair was curlier on one side than the other, so I decided to comb it. It became huge all over, so I sighed and put it into a ponytail. I dabbed some SPF 75 on my face and arms and I was ready. Before I walked to the Leaf, though, I logged on to the family computer.

**SCONE CONTEST LEADER BOARD**

1. Miss Cuppycake.........415 followers
2. Master Baker............311 followers
3. HaileyCakes.............295 followers
4. SweetCakes.............265 followers
5. PastrySwagger..........260 followers
6. Scone-y Nation.........216 followers

27. SteepingLeafScone.....19 followers

I knew that twenty-seventh place was at least a sign we were moving in the right direction, but there sure was a lot of work to do to become a real contender. I checked my blog to see if I had any new comments on my Parmesan berry scone post. It had two comments; not bad.

> **MadisonMom:** I loved your berry scone! I want to have another one at the teashop soon!
>
> July 28  6:27 a.m.
>
> **Miss Cuppycake:** I love cheesy scones. Very nice. ☺
>
> July 28  7:14 a.m.

I grinned. Mostly I was relieved there wasn't another mean comment from SweetCakes.

"Good morning, my dear! You're up early." Louisa waved as I approached the shop. She was outside on the patio tending to a small trellis of morning glories.

"Hi, Louisa. Yes, I guess I was just done sleeping. Nice day out here." I noticed that some of our chairs had dew on them, so I stepped inside to grab a towel. I came back out and began wiping them down.

"Thank you, dear, that was my next task," Louisa said. She watched me for a moment, and I could tell she was trying to decide if she should ask me about yesterday. I figured it couldn't hurt to ask her advice about Genna and Zoe. If only to avoid talking about Zach.

"So Gen and Zo got into a fight," I blurted out.

Louisa stopped trimming her plants and turned to me.

"Yeah. Genna doesn't want to eat normal food any-more. She's on a diet so she can look like this tiny actress or something. Zoe tried to talk her out of it, and now they're mad at each other."

"Oh dear. What won't she eat?" Louisa asked.

"You know, anything with, like, sugar in it." I tried to remember what else Genna had said. "She would only try a tiny bite of my bacon scone."

"I see." Louisa then said, almost to herself, "I wish people would think less about taking foods away and more about adding them in when they decide to change the way they eat."

"What do you mean?" I asked.

"Well, there is nothing wrong with making an effort to eat healthfully," Louisa replied. "We all probably *do* eat too much sugar, for example. It's just that often in our culture when a person wants to slim a bit, they decide to cut out everything they love to eat. They make food some sort of enemy, when really it's our lifelong friend. Every time I've made an effort to eat better, I try to *add* new foods. Then the ones that aren't serving me very well fade into the background for a while."

"Yeah. Maybe I can get Gen to talk to you," I said hopefully. "Like what new foods?"

"Hmm. Like quinoa or whole oats. Tahini, sushi, Chinese broccoli. All my favorites when I'm trying to lighten up a bit. Sometimes preparing these things takes more time, but that's part of honoring your body and the earth that has produced such goodness for you."

"Sounds tasty. Maybe I can get her to try some of those things."

"Good luck, dear. I know eating right isn't always easy. It's a very emotional thing for some people. But I'm sure you can be a helpful friend to Genna. Maybe all she needs is an example."

I thought about how I scarfed cupcakes and scones and realized I probably needed to shape up a bit if Genna was going to listen to me. Next time we had weekly tea, I vowed to make us some veggie sushi rolls with things from Zoe's garden. There was no way she could say no to that! I felt better already. It was so nice how when something was bothering me, Louisa always listened and had such good suggestions. I set down the towel I was using to wipe off the patio chairs and went over to give her a hug.

"I love you, Louisa," I said.

"Well! I love you too, Annie dear." She smiled at me. She looked happy but also wistful.

"What is it?" I asked.

"It's just that sometimes you remind me so much of your grandfather. Having you here at the shop reminds me of when we first opened. We spent a lot of time in between serving tea just chatting about our friends. And with them, of course."

"Sounds nice. And just like today," I added. I saw in Louisa's eyes her awareness of time going by. I wondered what it felt like, being a grandmother.

"Indeed." Louisa seemed to come back to the present then. She opened the Leaf's front door wide and propped it with a large pot containing a little banana tree with big leaves. I helped her to put out our sign on the sidewalk. It announced that the tea of the day would be French Breakfast.

Now that I had a plan to help Genna and Zoe, I debated whether to tell my grandmother about Zach. She always had the world's best advice, but I didn't want her to act any differently around him when he came back to the shop. Also, it was nice to have this thing that was all mine. I decided not to mention it for now. There were some things that were just too private to discuss. When Genna had shouted about it yesterday, I'd felt uneasy. Especially when she'd said the thing about me having a "real boyfriend" for high school. I looked down Monroe Street, both ways, hoping to see Zach standing on his bike, pedaling furiously toward me. All I saw was the mailman.

Since we were usually pretty quiet before eight a.m., I had some time to see if there were any comments on my blog entry about the bacon scone. I turned on Louisa's computer and waited. Finally, the scone contest page loaded and I checked the leader board. I was still near the bottom. I clicked on the first one, Sweet Impressions, and learned that she was the daughter of a cupcake-shop owner in San Francisco. Her latest recipe was for a lavender scone decorated with a real edible flower. Wow! I randomly clicked on the seventh. A blog page with the title Master Baker loaded. Its newest scone recipe appeared. I blinked. The title read "Cheesy Tomato Bacon Scone." It was almost EXACTLY the same as the one I had invented yesterday. A thin layer of sweat broke out on my forehead as I stared at the post. I reread it over and over. Not only was the post just like mine, but it had dozens of comments. All of a sudden my stomach began to ache, like it sometimes does when I get stressed out. How could this be?

Did the Steeping Leaf have a *spy*?

Dear readers,

I'm doing my best to create original scone recipes, but I'm worried there aren't enough ingredients to go around. I know it sounds silly, but I noticed that some of the other bakers in my scone competition have very similar recipes to mine and I can't help but stress about it. Making the same scone on the same day is *way worse* than wearing the same outfit to school on the same day as another girl. See, it only takes two minutes to change or throw on a different sweater, but it takes two HOURS to bake a scone. Do you know what I mean?

I need to invent a recipe that is so unusual no one could possibly think of it too. If you have any outrageous (and delicious) ideas, dear readers, PLZ message me.

Signed, freaking out,
Annie

July 28  7:52 a.m.

## Chapter Eight

It was fortunate that tea was at hand, to produce a lull and
provide refreshment . . .
—LOUISA MAY ALCOTT, *LITTLE WOMEN*

Master Baker's bacon scone recipe freaked
me out so much that I spent hours reading all of the other contestants' blogs.
Normally I would have *enjoyed* spending that much time
reading about delicious tea food, but instead I just felt
tense. I had new resolve to invent a truly original recipe
and get the Steeping Leaf blog into the top five. But
how could I get hundreds of new readers? The leader had
almost five hundred followers already. I had nineteen.

It was clearly time to get brainstorming.

And that meant it was list time.

I turned off the computer and went back out into the

shop. I grabbed a piece of paper and a pen from the cash register drawer and settled in at the counter. I explained to Louisa that we needed more blog followers, and fast. She said she'd be happy to offer a free cookie to our Internet fans.

## HOW TO GET 500 NEW BLOG FOLLOWERS IN LESS THAN ONE MONTH
### By Annie Green

1. Do a better job of publicizing the blog in the shop. More signs! Everywhere! In the bathrooms, on the chalkboard!

2. See if the Isthmus will do a blurb about the contest and the Steeping Leaf's plan to win.

3. Send an e-mail to everyone I've ever met asking them to follow the blog and comment on it. Also send an e-mail to everyone Louisa's ever met.

4. Hand out a flier with the link and a coupon for the Leaf.

5. Contact all the local pastry chefs in Madison for new scone ideas.

6. Have a baking demonstration at the farmer's market and ask people there to follow the blog.

7. *Get Genna and Zoe to help chalk again.*

8. *See if any other bloggers will link to the Steeping Leaf blog.*

9. *Comment on other people's blogs so they come check out ours.*

10. *Ask all the new little Teashop Girls for their help.*

11. *Post even more often so readers keep coming back (and share the blog with friends!).*

Whew! I knew I had some good ideas, but when I looked at the list, I saw how much work it would be. It made me happy to think that practically everything on there would also help business at the Leaf, though. And I loved the thought of meeting new people in Madison . . . especially pastry chefs! I wondered if they would talk to me.

I looked up from my list and saw that the shop was still pretty quiet. There was a mild breeze coming in through the open windows. Louisa was chatting with Ling and Hieu on the patio. I went out to say hello.

"Hieu, you're getting so big, buddy!" I knelt down to his level and was rewarded with a toothy grin. "Are you being good for your mama?"

"Occasionally," Ling said sweetly as she took a sip from the giant green tea frappe Louisa had prepared for her using matcha powder. Louisa stood up from their table just then and I saw her face light up. Mr. Arun had just arrived. He kissed my grandmother's cheek. Even though I'd seen him do it before, I still thought it was a tiny bit weird. I dropped my eyes involuntarily but quickly remembered my manners.

"Hello, Mr. Arun. Can I get you a pot of tea?" Louisa pulled out a chair for her sweetheart, and both Ling and Hieu said hello.

"Why, thank you, Annie. I would love a pot of peach ginger." It was still his favorite tea, all these months after the Teashop Girls had given him a sample at school. "But really, I can get it if you are busy." I assured him I wasn't and went to fetch the tea. Seeing my grandmother looking so girlishly happy around my former principal, I felt my heart speed up a bit when the thought of Zach once again popped into my head. This was getting ridiculous. It used to be that I would groan when he would crash through the door. Now I *wanted* him to? I didn't recognize myself.

I heard the door jingle and my head shot up. Seriously, this was crazy. After I delivered Mr. A's pot of tea, I decided to dust the shelves to distract myself. I pulled the stepladder out of the closet and placed it near the bookshelves.

"Hey, Annie," a familiar voice said. Genna! I didn't expect her to come in today.

"Gen! Hey! I'm glad to see you."

"Yeah. Um, sorry I sort of stormed off last night." She sounded sheepish, and kind of tired. I couldn't help but look at her with worry all over my face.

"That's okay. I'm just glad you came back. Should I call Zo?"

"Not yet. I'm still kind of mad at her for being so bossy," Genna said, putting her hands on her hips.

"She just wants to take care of you," I said.

"I suppose."

"You want some tea?" I decided not to press it, remembering my plan to make us all a special super-healthy treat for the next Teashop Girls tea. That would surely fix things up.

"Yeah, green please."

"You got it." I climbed down from the stepladder and went behind the counter. I grabbed a nice purple pot and scooped in one teaspoon of green tea. I poured in the hot water, and Gen and I grabbed a table. I showed her my latest list.

"See, I'm hundreds of followers behind right now, and I need to do something," I explained.

"These are great ideas, Annie. You're a totally natural, like, promoter," Genna said enthusiastically. She blew on her teacup and took several deep swallows. Her skin looked a little wan; I hoped the tea would perk her up.

"Thanks! I guess I am, but only when I have awesome things to tell people about." I smiled. It was true, I really enjoyed coming up with schemes and plans for the Leaf. It sure was more fun than homework.

"I want to help. I can design a flier for you and get my dad to print it at work. Can you write down the blog address again?"

"Wow. That would be amazing. Thank you." I quickly wrote down the URL on a Post-it. "Can you mention that the Leaf would give a free cookie to new blog followers who came in for a pot of tea?"

"Perfect. You want to go do some chalking now? I don't think it's supposed to rain this week," Genna said, and crossed her eyes. The last time we had tried it, the weather had *not* cooperated.

"Okay. Let me just tell Louisa I'm going to leave the shop for a bit." I took off my apron and went to look for some chalk.

Before we left the shop to decorate Monroe Street with the Leaf's URL, I added it to our sidewalk sign. Louisa said hello to Genna.

"It's nice to see you, dear. How are your parents?"

"They're good. They got me this," Gen said, and showed Louisa the latest smart phone.

"I have no idea what that is, sweetheart, but I'm sure it is wonderful," Louisa said with a smile.

"It is." Genna laughed. "We'll be back to finish my pot of tea soon!"

As soon as we were out of earshot of the Leaf's patio, Genna started grilling me about Zach. "Has he showed up yet? Did you talk to him last night?"

"Um, no," I said, a lot more calmly than I felt.

"Why not? You should call him!" She thrust her phone in my general direction. I didn't take it.

"I'd rather just, you know, see if he comes into the shop like usual," I said.

"Ooh, very smooth. Play it cool. I like it. I could've used your advice at camp," she added. I grinned. But the truth was, I had no idea what I was doing. It just seemed very weird to call Zach out of the blue when we only ever talked at the shop or at school. I wasn't being smooth, I was being chicken.

"Thanks," was all I said. It felt good having her think I was totally handling my new romantic developments like a pro.

"Should we start here?" she asked. It was as good a spot as any. I nodded.

In Genna's gorgeous looping handwriting the Monroe Street sidewalk said:

# Love the Leaf? Then love our blog!
## SteepingLeafScone.com

"Looks good," I said. "Genna, what's wrong?" After she had finished writing out the blog address, she had plopped down, right on the sidewalk. I couldn't believe she'd get her skirt dirty . . . it looked like it was vintage or from Anthropologie or some boutique on State Street. There were little flower shapes on it, hand-sewn. She squeezed her knees to her chest and rested her head on them.

"I'm just so . . . tired," she finally said in almost a whisper.

"Gen! I . . ." This had to be because she wasn't eating enough. But if I said something about it like Zoe had, would she storm off again? I decided I had to risk it. I couldn't pretend everything was fine when my usually bubbly friend was sitting on the ground like a lethargic cat. "I'm really worried about you. *Really.* You need to eat more food. You're probably dehydrated, too."

"I guess," was all she said. She pulled a bobby pin out of her hair and rolled it around in her fingers. I sat right down on the sidewalk with her and put my arm around her shoulder. "I haven't heard from James at all today. I feel awful," she added. She stuck the pin back in her hair and looked at her phone forlornly. I really, really, *really* wanted a cell phone. But at that moment I was kind of an eensy bit glad I didn't have one. It seemed like the whole world around Genna didn't matter at all if the little thing wasn't beeping every four seconds.

"Genna, maybe he's just busy. Please, please come back to the shop with me and let me make you lunch. It can even be a salad. Just so you eat something."

"Oh, all right." She was too low on energy to protest.

Relieved, I helped her to her feet and we headed back to the shop. Chalking could wait; I needed to take care of my best friend.

### Matcha Frappe

I've recently discovered the joy of powdered Japanese green tea, or matcha. It is LOADED with antioxidants and it is delicious. You buy it in little tins, but don't worry, you don't need much to make an incredible frappe. One tin of matcha is enough for dozens and dozens of marvelous, frothy, good-for-you drinks.

### Ingredients
1 cup ice
1 cup milk (I use 2%)
1 tablespoon sugar
½ teaspoon matcha powder

Add the ice, milk, and sugar to your blender, and blend on low until the mixture is nice and frothy. Add the matcha powder and blend on low for another minute. The drink will be a lovely green color. Makes one shake. Enjoy!

July 28  11:31 p.m.

## Chapter Nine

The cup of tea on arrival at a country house is a thing which, as a rule, I particularly enjoy. I like the crackling logs, the shaded lights, the scent of buttered toast, the general atmosphere of leisured cosiness.
—P. G. WODEHOUSE, *THE CODE OF THE WOOSTERS*

The next day, after I helped open the shop and had a huge pot of Irish Breakfast tea with milk and sugar, I told Louisa I'd be in the Leaf office for most of the morning. I spent a *lot* of time sending messages to people about the Steeping Leaf's new blog. Next, I visited lots and lots of food blogs and commented on them, hoping they'd come and read my posts in return. I kept checking the leader board, and sure enough, my efforts bumped us up a couple of slots! I visited SweetCakes's blog and saw that she had just baked a blueberry walnut scone. It didn't seem that interesting, but I had to admit that her photos were very nice.

You could really see the blueberries and the texture of the scone itself. I needed to take more close-ups. Back at the SteepingLeafScone.com blog, I saw that I had FOUR comments for my bacon scone post. Yay!

**MickeysGrrrl:** World's Greatest Scone ☺
July 29  6:11 a.m.

**REALfoodie:** Nice job with these. I love savory scones.
July 29  7:22 a.m.

**Scone-y Nation:** Hey, Steeping Leaf, these look fantastic. I bet they taste really great.
July 29  7:46 a.m.

**Anonymous:** MMMM BACON.
July 29  8:02 a.m.

I giggled. People *love* bacon. In anything.

**SCONE CONTEST LEADER BOARD**

1. Master Baker............478 followers
2. Miss Cuppycake.........472 followers
3. PastrySwagger..........454 followers
4. Scone-y Nation.........401 followers
5. SweetCakes.............390 followers

## 23. SteepingLeafScone.........45 followers

The blog was chugging along and I was feeling better about Genna. I was really worried when she nearly passed out during our sidewalk chalking, but she had eaten every last bit of the lunch I'd fixed for her and promised me that she would be more careful. We'd had a long talk, and she confessed that she had been going to super-intense spinning classes every day and only consuming beet and carrot juice instead of regular food. I said I thought it would be a good idea if she got rid of all her glossy celebrity magazines. Seeing Cecily Stevens every day was making her so unhappy. Sure, I liked looking at the cute vampire boys as much as she did. But it wasn't worth it if it ultimately made you feel miserable.

We settled on her agreeing to eat at least one meal at the Leaf each day. In return I promised that the food Louisa and I fixed for her would be nutritious and not loaded with sugar or butter. Then I went over to the Leaf bookshelves and lent her some good books. I figured if she got absorbed by *I Capture the Castle*, she might forget about her celeb rags for a little while. It was the best I could do. I told myself—and Genna—that if she had one more episode like the one on the sidewalk, I was going straight to my mom, who would call a doctor. That made her mad, but she said okay. I felt proud of myself. I knew that when it came to clothes and boys, I was a clueless freak show. But I could take care of my friends.

As soon as Genna got the fliers printed, the blog would really take off, I just knew it. It was definitely time for a new post. I'd been thinking about doing a cookies and cream scone, but before I could blog it, I had to make it.

First, I walked down the street to Zuzu Café and Market for some organic cookies. Then I preheated the oven and started making my scone base.

"Ooh, what do we have here, dear?" Louisa asked. The shop was busy, so I kept taking breaks from mixing my batter to fetch chais and pots of tea. I didn't mind. It was nice to see most of the tables all full.

"It's going to be a cookies and cream scone," I said. "I think it'll be a popular one." I put some of the cookies on a cutting board and used a spoon to break them up into small pieces.

"I love it! And it's the perfect day for them too," Louisa said. "We have lots of young customers. It's too bad Mr. Silverman is still in Europe, I bet he'd adore these."

I looked around and noticed it was true. The shop was full of kids. I was glad I decided on a sweet scone. Mr. Silverman was in Paris for a month; we'd gotten a lovely postcard from him the week before. I made a mental note to send him a letter . . . surely blog followers in Europe counted?

When the batter was ready, I added the cookie pieces and the secret ingredient. Then I cut the dough into little triangles, brushed them with milk, and placed the pan in the oven.

As focused as I was on the scone prep, I couldn't help but look at the door. Where was Zach? I was less jumpy than yesterday, but still confused. Before our storage room kiss, I'd seem him practically every single day. Most times *twice* a day. Had I done something wrong? Were my lips too dry? I fished a Chapstick out of my Leaf apron and put some on.

Just then, the Leaf's door jingled. I glanced up to see Genna bounding into the shop. She looked so much better than she had the day before. She wore navy blue short shorts with big white polka dots and a bright tangerine blouse. On her feet were flats covered in white sequins. Both of her hands were full of papers.

"I've got them!" she exclaimed. "Fliers for the blog!"

"Hello, dear." Louisa smiled. "How delightful!"

"Hi, Louisa. I made these last night and my dad printed them up this morning. Aren't they cute?" Genna handed me a stack of several hundred fliers. I was thrilled!

"They look wonderful, darling. You are a very talented

artist," Louisa replied. It was true. Genna had done a beautiful illustration of a plate of scones for the flier. They looked good enough to eat. She included the link for the Steeping Leaf blog. And it doubled as a coupon. "Let's hand them out right away."

We made sure every table in the shop and on the patio got some fliers. Lots of the newest Teashop Girls were very excited and took extra fliers to give to their friends. I knew they would be a big help, because I'd worked hard earlier in the summer to make sure all the young girls who came into the Leaf got pink Teashop Girls buttons and loyalty punch cards. Not only were their cards good for free pots of tea on their birthdays, but we also sometimes gave away cute prizes and things. Everyone thought it was the best club ever. I mentioned to them that my latest scones were almost done. If they stayed at the shop a bit longer, they could try one.

"Annie?" One girl tugged at my yellow apron. She looked about six. She was with her mom, who smiled at me. I think the girl's name was Greta, but I wasn't sure.

"Yes?"

"What's a scone?"

I smiled. I'd never really explained it to everyone because I think I might have been born knowing. "Is your name Greta?" I asked first.

"Yes. It is spelled G-R-E-T-A! I'm six," she added.

"Very nice. Well, Greta, a scone is a kind of little bread, or cake, if it has sugar. It was invented in Scotland, which is part of the United Kingdom. Have you ever heard of that?"

"Um, um, no . . . maybe." She looked at her mom, who whispered to her that Harry Potter lived in the United Kingdom. "Yes!"

"Well, anyway, scones are little delicious treats that people have with tea. You can put jam or clotted cream on them. Or both, like I do."

"Okay. Thank you, Annie Green."

I thought it was adorable that all the younger girls who came into the shop knew my name. I tried to give them extra-attentive service and make sure that they found a tea they would love. It was my favorite part of the job.

When Louisa went outside with a fresh pot of hot water, I handed Genna a plate I'd made up earlier with hummus, veggies, kalamata olives, and whole wheat pita bread. She grinned and put a baby carrot in her mouth. "Thanks, Annie. But actually, you'll be happy to know I had a big breakfast—a smoothie AND two eggs. I feel amazing. Where is Zach?"

"I don't know," I said quietly. "I guess he's busy this week."

"We should go find him," she suggested. Her eyes glimmered; Genna *loved* potential romantic drama, no matter whose. "Maybe he's on foursquare, I'll check." She immediately began working her phone with her thumbs.

"Um," was all I replied. I didn't know what she meant, but even so, the idea made my stomach flip. I knew Zach played Ultimate Frisbee a lot; maybe we could go get Zoe and have tea in the park. Then if we ran into him . . . it might be fun.

"C'mon, Annie. After the scones are done."

"Okay. I'm calling Zoe, though." If I was going to run into Zach on purpose, it would be easier with my two best friends at my side.

"I already did," Genna said quickly, looking embarrassed. "She's not home."

"Oh. Well, I'm glad you called." I felt relieved. Maybe things between Gen and Zo were already okay.

"Yeah. Hey, I think your scones are done." Genna was right, I could smell them. I took them out of the oven to cool. Several little girls came up to the counter to sniff them. I said it would just be a couple more minutes. I turned the fan toward the plate to speed things up.

Genna helped me to hand the scones out. Everyone loved them . . . it was going to be so hard to choose which to bake if we made it to Chicago!

"Annie! Annie!" one little girl shouted. "This is the best thing I have ever tasted!"

"Thank you!" I said. "I'm glad you like it."

"It is really good," her mom said with a wink. I handed out extra napkins all around the shop.

At another table a brother and sister each had one. "I would eat this every single day," the boy said.

"Yes, for breakfast and for lunch and for dinner," his sister said.

"Well, you might get sick of it after a week," I told them with a smile. I knew they were just excited to get an unexpected treat, but the soft scone was indeed nicely improved by the crunchy chocolate cookies. And the vanilla bean filling melted in, making the scone extra creamy. Yum!

When the shop settled back down, Genna informed Louisa I needed a long break.

"Is it okay if I kidnap Annie for a walk to Vilas Park?" she asked, a glint in her eye.

"Of course, dear! It's a gorgeous day. Let me pack you a picnic."

"Ooh, you don't have to. We're just going for a little bit."

"I insist, my lovelies. It's too nice outside to hurry back. You could sit on that walking bridge and feed the ducks when you're done eating."

Genna giggled. "Sounds . . . romantic." I crossed my eyes at her, knowing immediately that she had a romantic duck-feeding situation with Zach in mind for me.

Louisa packed a small basket for us with iced teas, grapes, and egg-salad sandwiches on whole wheat. She winked at me on our way out, and I winked back. I knew she'd packed a healthy lunch with Genna in mind. Louisa was the best grandmother ever.

At the park we spread out our blanket near the tennis courts. Genna ate her sandwich and drank her tea, and we shared the grapes. We didn't see any sign of Zach, but it was nice to lie in the sun for a bit. I hoped I hadn't missed any spots on my legs when I'd put on sunscreen earlier this morning.

"Annie! There he is!" Genna sat up and pointed.

"Where? Oh yeah." Zach was racing across the open grass in pursuit of a Frisbee. It went into the nearby pond and he went in after it. Gross.

I didn't know what to do. Was I supposed to go over there and say hi? I suddenly wished I'd stayed at the Leaf, where things were predictable.

"Go over there!" Genna said. "Say hello."

"But they're in the middle of the game."

"No, I think they're taking a break. Look."

Much to my dismay, they did seem to be quitting. I

saw several players ambling back to their piles of stuff near the field sidelines. It looked for a moment like Zach was coming toward us, but then he started heading to the zoo instead. He hadn't seen me. It wasn't too late to leave the park. But instead I decided to be bold for a change and stood up. Genna clapped.

"You're coming with me," I said. I pulled the sparkly lip gloss out of my pocket and put some on.

"Fine." She stood up and we walked, as casually as possible, in Zach's direction. When we caught up to him, Genna poked him in the back. I wanted to disappear, but it was too late.

"Hey, loser," she said.

"Genna Matthews, my favorite Teashop Girl. And Annie Green, who must be on a special work-release program."

*What? How could* Genna *be his favorite?* I opened my mouth to speak, but nothing came out.

"Zach, where have you been?" Genna asked impatiently. I could tell his remark had flustered her, too.

"Aw, did you miss me?" he said to me.

"Actually, the Steeping Leaf smells one hundred percent better without you in it," I managed to sputter. If he was going to be mean, I could play that game too.

"Sure, if you like the aroma of dusty antiques," he

replied. I watched his face carefully. Other than blinking more than usual, he was the same old annoying Zach. I guessed whatever had happened between us didn't mean anything. Fine. I crossed my arms and told Genna I should get back to work. She shot him a look and we walked back to our picnic.

As we were walking away, Zach said, super quietly, "Wait." I turned around. He said, "Nothing." I kept walking with Genna because I couldn't think of what else to do. I wanted to stick out my tongue at him, but I felt too old to do that. What was the high school equivalent of sticking out your tongue?

"Sorry, Annie. I think he's just too immature to be boyfriend material," Genna said. "Maybe we should go to the mall and see if there are any cute boys there."

"No thanks, Gen," I said quietly. I kept my face down for a few moments so she wouldn't notice that my eyes had tears in them.

# SteepingLeafScone.com

Dear readers,

Check out the beautiful flier that Genna made to help me promote my blog and get more local readers! I love it!

## Have you heard about Madison's newest and <u>BEST</u> food blog?

You've enjoyed the treats at the Steeping Leaf for ages!
Now learn how Annie and Louisa make their magic.
By following the blog, you'll be helping the Leaf become
a finalist in a baking competition!

### www.SteepingLeafScone.com

Follow our blog and present this flier at the Steeping Leaf
for a free cookie when you purchase a pot of tea
through August 30th.

<3 Annie

## Chapter Ten

One sip of this will bathe the drooping spirits in delight,
beyond the bliss of dreams.
—JOHN MILTON

Back at the Leaf, things were quieter than they'd been all morning. Louisa said she could use a nap, so I said I'd watch the front. She often took little siestas around two p.m., so I knew that when it was time for me to go back to school in the fall, we'd need to hire a new barista—regardless of the outcome of the scone contest.

I felt bad about the way Zach had acted, and worse that it mattered so much to me. It wasn't that I expected him to completely change personalities and be *nice* all of the sudden. But it seemed like he was deliberately trying to hurt my feelings by calling Genna his favorite Teashop

Girl. I knew that he and I weren't *friends*, exactly, but I thought we were something. Even before the stupid kiss. It was so, so confusing and dumb.

I sighed and decided to work on the blog some more. I couldn't do it from the computer in the back room when I was supposed to be watching the front of the store, so I called home and asked Beth if I could borrow her laptop. My parents had gotten her one for college, but I knew she was supposed to share it with me before she left. She said I could and even offered to bring it to the shop. I was touched. Beth had gotten a lot nicer over the summer. I think she was secretly scared to leave home, now that college was just around the corner instead of in the distant future.

"Don't spill any tea on it," she warned when she walked it over. I made her a really tasty chai latte in a to-go cup as thanks.

"I won't," I promised. "Hey, Beth?"

"Yeah?"

I wanted to ask her for boy advice, but something made me stop. Maybe I was worried she'd tease me; maybe I was worried that telling more people what happened would mean I'd have to do something about it. "Can you ask your friends to follow my blog? It's important."

I hadn't asked her earlier. I spent so much time at the Leaf these days that I barely even saw my sister. I made a mental note to try to find some quality time to spend with her before she moved away; I felt a little guilty about being so excited to have more bathroom time. I knew I would actually miss her when she was gone.

"Sure. I'll tell them tonight; we're all going to the Orpheum for a show."

"Thanks, B. See you later."

I found an unsecure wireless signal from a neighbor and posted the cookies and cream scone recipe to the blog.

Next, I spent some time commenting on other blogs. I made the rounds of all the contestants at the top of the leader board (and said nice things to everyone but SweetCakes), some tea blogs that I've been following for a long time, and some local blogs written by people here in Madison. I always read the blogger's entire post and tried to add a thoughtful comment. I didn't outright ask for anyone to go to my blog, but I always linked to it. This kind of thing seemed pretty common, so I didn't feel like I was making a nuisance of myself. After about half an hour I returned to see if anyone had read my new post. There was already one comment! I clicked on it.

**SweetCakes:** Secret ingredient? I'm sure it's TEA. Lame-o. Try again, Steeping Leaf.

July 29  1:37 p.m.

AUGHHHHHHHHHHH, SWEETCAKES!

Not again. My Internet flamer was back, and worse than ever. I stared at the comment in horror. It was *really* starting to feel like we had a spy. Who had seen me add my secret ingredient? I glanced around the shop, half convinced I would see a camera somewhere.

I couldn't believe my secret ingredient wasn't a secret anymore. I felt so helpless. There wasn't even anyone in the shop I could show the comment to. I quickly shut down the computer, as if I could get the insult to go away by not looking at it. I angrily did some dishes and decided that from now on, I'd bake only after hours, when no one could see what I was doing.

What a rotten day.

After a little while I settled down and got bored, so I signed back on, hoping Zoe or Genna would be home now. I saw Zoe's dot turn green on chat, and immediately messaged her.

**cuppaAnnie:** I think there's a scone spy at the Leaf
**Kswiss211:** What?

**cuppaAnnie:** Yes. One of my rivals just posted my secret ingredient in the comments.
**Kswiss211:** oh noes!
**cuppaAnnie:** and, I went to go look for Zach and he was so mean. ☹
**Kswiss211:** yuck. Should I come visit you?
**cuppaAnnie:** yes. Oh good news, tho. Gen ate lunch.
**Kswiss211:** good. C u in a min.
**cuppaAnnie:** l8r

I felt better now that I knew Zoe was coming to visit me, so I spent a few minutes getting my blog listed on different websites and stuff. I registered with the Food Lovers Blogroll and added a blogroll to my own blog. That way, I could link up with the blogs I had already visited. I also e-mailed the reporter at the *Isthmus* who'd covered our anniversary party. Maybe she'd do a blurb about my blog and our efforts to get to London. I checked the leader board again. SweetCakes was in fourth place, and SteepingLeafScone.com was in nineteenth. So unfair. I checked the contest rules to see if they could be disqualified for being rude, but it didn't look like they could be. You could only get disqualified for:

1. Being over the age of sixteen on September 1 of this year;
2. Having blog followers who were not real people;

3. Hiring a professional photographer to take the
   food photos.

Zoe came through the door in her tennis whites.

"Hey, Annie. Where is Louisa?" she asked.

"Napping in the hammock in the garden. She calls it
her 'business hammock.'"

"Oh. Cool. So let's see it—I can't stay very long." I
turned the screen toward her and she gasped.

"I know," I said. "And this is the second mean one
SweetCakes has left on the site!"

"Can I try something?" Zoe asked. She reached for
the laptop, and I gave it to her. "I'm going to see where
SweetCakes posts from. Sometimes you can tell by the
IP address."

"Okay. Their blog doesn't say. I don't think they have
a shop or restaurant."

"Hmm. I can't find anything. It's like they were able to
block the address stamp. Could be someone here, could be
someone in a different state. How annoying! You know, you
could log in to your account and just delete the comment."

"I guess. But it would only egg her on. Plus, I want
all the other contestants to see how mean SweetCakes is
being."

"Yeah. Blarg."

"You can say that again. I hope we can still win, even if our secret ingredient isn't a secret."

"We can." Zoe carefully set the computer down and put her arm around my shoulder. "Your scones are delicious. And I saw the fliers. Beautiful!"

"Thanks."

"Oh, I almost forgot. I brought you some more produce from the garden." Zoe started digging in her tote bag and pulled out some more tomatoes, cucumbers, and raspberries. "You can use them for Leaf finger sandwiches or for the scones. I'm thinking of trying to get some of this stuff into the school cafeterias around Madison. What do you think?"

"I think it's a great idea!" I said. I rinsed a raspberry and popped it into my mouth.

"Will you help me send a letter and some information to the school-board members? I was doing some research, and even though Madison has better lunches than some districts, there's still a lot more we could do. Like, why is it so hard to serve green salads? Kids should get used to having greens every day."

"Sure, I can help out. But promise me you'll make up with Genna. I'm going to put together veggie sushi rolls for tea tomorrow. She'll love them. And it wouldn't kill me to eat healthier either."

"I promise." Zoe looked at her watch. "I have to go, my parents have early dinner reservations for us. We can work on the school-board letter tomorrow."

"Sounds good."

I made a pot of jasmine pearls and added some cool-looking widgets to my blog. A lot of my competitors did videos and really sophisticated photos. I wondered if I should try something like that. It wouldn't hurt to make the food look as glorious as possible. I dug around Louisa's cupboards and pulled out some pretty table-cloths. The next time I took photos, I'd have a special background for the scone tiers. I dug deeper into the cupboards to see if there were any special antique dishes I should be using. Every little bit would help.

The little bell on the front door jingled, and I popped my head out of the linen cabinet.

*Zach.*

"Sorry, Zach, Genna's not here." I frowned.

"Genna? What? Oh yeah. No, that's okay." He sounded different than he had earlier. Quieter.

"What do you want?"

"Nothing. I was just seeing if you needed any help . . . you know, making a scone thing. Or whatever." He looked down at his feet.

"I already made one today. Here." I handed Zach a

cookies and cream scone. I realized that I couldn't withhold Steeping Leaf yumminess from anyone, not even Zach. I really *was* an excellent barista. He ate it in two bites.

"That was terrible," he said, but grinned as he said it. I couldn't help it; I smiled a teeny bit too.

"I know. You want another one?"

"Yes." He took one and ate it the same way, as if he hadn't been fed in a year. "You're a horrible cook."

"Shut it, mutant."

The air between us had changed somehow and we both relaxed. I felt better, like things were a little more normal. I know what you're thinking; I was being *waaay* too nice. But I couldn't help but remember all the helpful things Zach had done around the shop before things went south. He'd helped Louisa fix a shelf at the beginning of the summer. He'd noticed that the windowsills had spiderwebs and had climbed up and cleaned them off. Of course, when I had seen him dangling practically from the roof like a monkey when he was doing it, I'd yelled my head off. Thinking about days like that helped me to brush off his obnoxious side.

"So, is there tea in this one too?" he asked casually. I jumped.

"What? *You* know the secret ingredient? YOU'RE THE SCONE SPY!"

"What are you talking about? Anyone with half a brain could guess—"

"GET OUT!" I came around the counter and pushed Zach out of the Leaf.

"Annie, stop it. C'mon!"

I gave him one final push and then closed the door. And locked it. Why did I *ever* think it was a good idea to be nice to Zach? He was nothing but problems.

## To Do: Wednesday, July 30

- Come up with new secret ingredient.
- Make Zach sorry he was born.
- Make sure Gen and Zo make up because we're setting an example for new Teashop Girls now.
- Get more blog followers.
- Help Zo get decent greens and stuff into school cafeterias.

**Cookies & Cream Scones**

This scone is inspired by my favorite kind of ice cream, the Chocolate Shoppe's cookies and cream flavor. It's the perfect scone to have with a rich black tea like English Breakfast. I hope you love it . . . it might be my favorite recipe so far!

**Ingredients**

2 cups all-purpose flour

1 tablespoon baking powder

¾ cup sugar

½ teaspoon salt

3 tablespoons butter

1 egg

1 cup chopped chocolate sandwich cookies

½ cup buttermilk

½ teaspoon secret ingredient

¼ cup milk

Preheat the oven to 400 degrees Fahrenheit. Mix the dry ingredients together first, then cut in the butter. Stir in the beaten egg and the cookie pieces. Slowly add the buttermilk to form a thick dough. Add the secret ingredient. Knead the dough on a board, roll to a 1-inch thickness, and cut the dough into 2-inch rounds. Place each round on a greased cookie sheet and brush the tops with milk. Bake for about 12 to 15 minutes until golden brown; serve warm. Makes 12 scones.

**Customer comments:**

"This is the best thing I've ever eaten." "I would eat [these scones] every day!"

July 29  7:12 p.m.

## Chapter Eleven

Closing my eyes, I find green mountains and pure water within my
own heart. Silently sitting alone and drinking tea,
I feel these become a part of me.
—Soshitsu Sen, Grand Master XIV, Urasenke School of Tea

The next morning, I didn't go right to the
Leaf. Instead I put on my oldest jeans, a
T-shirt from fifth-grade graduation, and
beat-up sneakers with grass stains. I tied my hair back
with a yellow cotton scarf and slathered on sunscreen and
bug spray. Zoe had invited Genna and me to her garden!

The plot that Zoe tended was about 15 by 15 feet. It
doesn't sound that big, but there was *so* much growing
there. Genna arrived right after me, and we found Zoe
with her hands in the dirt already. Actually, she was stirring some soil in a big wooden bin in the corner of the
plot with a small hoe. It was funny seeing my friend, who

was usually the epitome of neatness and crisp white tennis clothing, working in the dirt. It suited her, though. It occurred to me that maybe her neatness had less to do with *her* and more to do with what her parents expected. Was the real Zoe the one with dirt under her fingernails?

"Hey, Zo, what are you doing?" I asked.

"Hey! I'm working on our compost bin. See, you add all your leftover food garbage, and we have these special worms that turn it into rich soil. It's really good for the plants."

"Cool," Genna said appreciatively.

"Louisa has one too," I said. "You can put used tea leaves in compost bins!"

"That's totally true. And coffee grounds. Let me show you our green beans." Zoe grinned. "They're ripe. And delicious." A trellis rose along the southern border of the plot. It was indeed chock full of beans. Zoe pulled off a few and handed them to us.

Genna and I popped the beans into our mouths. They were tasty. Almost like candy, they were so sweet.

"Zo . . . ," Gen began. I could tell she was going to say something important, because she sounded very serious. "I'm sorry about how I acted at tea the other day."

Zoe hugged Genna. "I just want you to be healthy."

"I know. I want that too. And it doesn't matter about

Cecily anyway. I talked to James on the phone last night, and he says he doesn't even want to be friends with her anymore because she's, like, a *total* diva."

We all laughed. Genna popped some more beans into her mouth.

"Actually, I feel kind of bad for her," Gen said thoughtfully. "It's no fun being hungry. And I bet she doesn't have friends like I do."

"Aw, Genna. You're making me all *verklempt*." Zoe fanned her face and I laughed.

"I'm going to make us veggie sushi for tea later," I said. "Let's pick what we want in it!"

Zoe pulled a carrot out of the ground. Genna chose a ripe tomato and a cucumber. I cut some cilantro. We put the vegetables and fresh herbs in Zoe's bag. Then we helped her weed and water all of the plants. The sun was so bright you could practically feel their leaves growing. I was definitely going to come out and help Zoe more often. I loved Louisa's flower garden too, but standing in the middle of this sort of plot and getting to snack while you worked was really cool. I inspected the raspberry patch and popped a few berries into my mouth. *Mmm!*

I thought about food and how it could be pretty complicated. It was something you could share with friends and family, something you could love and even grow yourself. But I also knew that for many people, food could cause a lot of stress. If you ate too much of the wrong kinds, it could also cause bad health. The cookies and cream scones were awesome, but I wanted my next scone to be delicious and also nutritious.

I also hoped that Genna wouldn't try any more extreme diets. I needed all the taste testers I could get! I thought about Zach's little visit and frowned.

"I think Zach has been spying on my scone baking and giving my secrets to the competition," I said as we were packing up.

"Zach?" Zoe said, surprised. "He would," Genna said at the exact same time.

"Yeah."

"He must be punished," Zoe said. All three of us nodded and headed for the Leaf.

## 4 Ways to Punish Zach for Being a Scone Spy and General Pain in the Neck

1. Hide his bike.
2. Take a picture of him drinking tea with his pinky extended and put it on the Internet.

3. *Tell his Ultimate Frisbee team he has a contagious rash from swimming in the lake.*

"Ew!" I said. "Genna, how come you always come up with the meanest ones? Remind me not to get on your bad side."

"It's just a talent of mine," she said with a giggle. "You should hear some of the things understudies plot to do to the leads of plays to get onstage."

"Annie," Zoe said mischievously, "you better hope Zach doesn't actually have a rash from algae. You hang out with him more than anyone."

"I do not!" I cried. "And I'm definitely not going to let him into the Leaf from now on."

Genna and Zoe both laughed at me. I blushed and jabbed them both with my elbows as we walked. They squealed and jumped away. The next item on the list was my idea.

4. *Refuse to give him any more free, delicious food at the Leaf.*

Dear readers,

Today we have a special treat. My BFF Zoe has been volunteering at a community garden all summer, and she's helping me learn about when certain fruits and vegetables reach their peak ripeness so they'll be extra delicious when you bake or cook with them.

You'll notice the offerings at your farmer's market change as the summer goes on. Which seasonal fruit or veggie would you like to see me bake with next??

**Zoe's Seasonal Produce List of Yumminess**

**May:** basil, asparagus, sugar snap peas

**June:** cherries, melons, apricots, spinach, blueberries

**July:** corn, peaches, strawberries, beets, green beans, raspberries

**August:** tomatoes, grapes, zucchini, watermelon

**September:** apples, pears, wild mushrooms, cranberries

<3 Annie

July 30  8:32 a.m.

## Chapter Twelve

I expect I shall feel better after tea.
—P. G. WODEHOUSE, *CARRY ON, JEEVES*

I f you ever have boy trouble, I recommend having tea with your friends. It's the perfect thing to do, because it's fun *and* it requires a little planning. The planning takes your mind off the boy, and the actual tea is so pleasant, you'll practically forget you ever even met him. Even if he is *spying* on you to make sure you don't get to go to London. Which, if you ask me, has got to be the worst possible thing a person could do to you.

Anyway, after Genna and Zoe and I arrived at the Leaf, I got busy planning our tea. Zoe disappeared into the bathroom and came out looking immaculate. She must carry a hairbrush in her bag, because her hair was smoother than silk. Okay, so maybe she really *did* enjoy being clean.

"Louisa, can I use your sushi kit?"

"Of course, darling." She finished blending up a matcha green tea shake with soy milk for Mr. Kopinski and tapped her finger against her chin. "If I can remember where I hid it last time," she said with a smile. "Hello, girls."

"Hi, Louisa," Genna and Zoe said in unison. "I like this music," Genna said. "What is it?"

"Thank you, dear. It's Billie Holiday," Louisa said. She'd recently purchased a record player at a garage sale and we had it set up in one corner of the shop. She said it was just like one she'd had as a girl. I'd never used one before, but I was getting good at carefully placing the needle down on the albums. I really liked the rich, scratchy sound of some of Louisa's ancient records. It made the shop feel even more lush and inviting.

My grandmother disappeared into the back for a moment in a waft of scarves and tinkling jewelry and returned with the kit, which had a special bamboo rolling mat. Louisa spent so much time at her shop that even though sushi wasn't on the menu, she kept a rice steamer here for her own personal use. She also always kept nori around. Nori is paper-thin green seaweed. It sounds kind of strange, but it tastes really good. It forms the outside of the roll and holds everything together. I got the rice started and pulled out a cutting board to cut up the vegetables into perfect long pieces for my rolls.

"Can I check and see where SteepingLeafScone.com is in the contest rankings?" Zoe asked.

"Yeah!" Genna said. "Let's!"

"Sure," I said. "You can use the computer in back. It takes a while, but when you open up the Web browser, I have the rankings set as my home page so it will come right up."

"Cool." They both walked back there as I finished my slicing. This was only the second time I'd made sushi, so I wanted Louisa to stay nearby. She's the one who taught me how to do it, of course. My mom says sushi is too much work. And my dad says he prefers his food cooked. Beth loves it, though.

"It looks like everyone is simpatico again," Louisa said. She sipped the leftovers from the matcha shake she'd just made.

"I think so," I said with a smile. "Thank goodness. That mean blog commenter is back, so I'm going to really need Gen and Zo to help us win the contest."

"What did the commenter say?" Louisa asked, mystified. She never used the Internet for anything other than e-mailing her friends in different cities.

"She—or he, I really have no idea—knows that our secret ingredient is tea." I started slicing my vegetables more vehemently, and Louisa gently took the knife away from me and calmly continued the task herself. I wiped my hands clean and began pulling out some small square plates for us to use.

"Hmm. That's too bad." Louisa didn't sound nearly angry enough for my taste. But then again, she never sounded angry.

"Yes. It *is* too bad. I think we have a spy. I'm going to have to quit baking when customers are around. Especially Zach Anderson." I checked the rice and pulled some soy sauce out of the little refrigerator.

I could tell Louisa was about to protest, but fortunately, she was interrupted by Genna and Zoe, who bounced out of the back room with big smiles on their faces.

"Good news! SteepingLeafScone.com has lots of new followers since yesterday," Zoe said.

"Seventy-five, to be exact," Genna chimed in. "You're up to thirteenth place. Not bad for one day!"

I grinned. Seventy-five new followers? Wow! I guess all of the e-mailing and fliers had worked. I knew my blog wasn't nearly as fancy as some of the others, but I also knew that lots of Madisonians loved the Steeping Leaf and were supporting us now. Yay!

"Wait. What about SweetCakes?" I asked in a low voice. "Are they still in fourth?"

Louisa interrupted. "Don't worry about SweetCakes, Teashop Girls. SweetCakes is on one path, and we are on another. What is *our* path?" I smiled a bit ruefully. Louisa always liked to bring a little Zen into the discussion when I'd prefer to be anything but.

"Our path is delicious!" Zoe said, taking the bait.

"Righteous!" Genna added with a fist pump.

"Our path goes to London," I finished up. All of us high-fived.

**Veggie Sushi**

**Ingredients**

4 cups water

2 cups short-grain white rice

1 cucumber

1 avocado

½ cup rice vinegar

4 tablespoons brown sugar

1 package of pre-toasted nori sheets

½ cup soy sauce

1 tablespoon prepared wasabi paste

Bring the water to a boil and add the rice. Lower to a simmer and let cook for about 35 minutes. Peel and cut the cucumber and avocado up into small strips; set aside. Mix the vinegar and brown sugar together and add to the rice once it is finished. Let the rice mixture cool.

Lay out a nori sheet on a clean surface or bamboo mat. Put a clump of rice the size of a small apple in the center of the sheet and use your hand to press the rice to the edges of the sheet so it covers the whole thing. It works best if you keep your hands moist while you're doing this. Next, place a row of sliced cucumber and avocado pieces in the center of the sheet and firmly roll the nori into a tight roll. Slice the roll into 6 pieces. Repeat with all nori sheets. Makes 4 to 5 rolls.

Serve the sushi pieces with soy sauce and wasabi paste.

July 30  2:06 p.m.

## Chapter Thirteen

I shouldn't think even millionaires could eat anything nicer than
new bread and real butter and honey for tea.
—DODIE SMITH

After we finished our late afternoon sushi tea
party, Genna noticed that Louisa was rewrit-
ing the Steeping Leaf food menu. We were
keeping our classics like cucumber sandwiches with the
crusts cut off, but Louisa was adding some more healthy
offerings as well. One of the new items would be a small
wheat berry salad with green apples, raisins, almonds, and
cinnamon.

"What's a wheat berry?" Genna asked as she helped me
dry our tea dishes. Zoe had to leave for a tennis lesson,
but Gen stayed behind to help us close up the shop for
the day.

"It's a whole wheat kernel," Louisa explained. "They're very tasty . . . kind of chewy and full of fiber."

"Interesting. Do you think I could maybe go to the grocery store with you sometime?" Genna asked.

"Of course, dear. But I don't really go to the grocery store that often. I go to the co-op and to the farmer's market, and to the smaller stores."

"That's okay. I just want to learn more about your birdseed." Genna grinned. Louisa ruffled her hair, which was piled on her head and arranged in an interesting pattern of bobby pins.

I thought about what Louisa had said regarding adding foods instead of taking them away when you were trying to "lighten up," as she said. I'd always kind of dismissed her wheat berries and other unfamiliar things as "Louisa's weird health food," but now I wanted to know more too. I'd have to, if I was going to come up with a scone recipe that was both award-winning *and* healthy.

"Can I come too?" I asked.

"Yes, dear. Why don't we lock up a bit early and take a little field trip right now?" Genna and I nodded eagerly. When the shop was all clean, the sign pulled in, and the doors secure, we hopped into my grandmother's old truck and headed for the store.

When we were there, Louisa explained that she'd load

up the cart with her normal staples. If we didn't recognize something, we should just ask and we could try it later.

Genna and I started not recognizing things right away.

"What's that?" Gen asked when Louisa put a smooth, fat yellow tube in the cart.

"Polenta," she replied. "It's boiled cornmeal. Very good with shitaki mushrooms and a little olive oil and Parmesan."

"Are you a vegetarian?" Genna asked.

"No, but I don't eat much meat. I have some maybe once or twice per week. Usually fish. If you're interested in becoming one, though, I have some books you can read. It is very important to become educated about protein and getting enough iron and B vitamins if you decide to skip meat."

"Okay." Genna sounded impressed. We continued to follow Louisa around the store as she added lots of vegetables to her cart. Fortunately, we recognized most of them. Some of the mushrooms she picked out looked a bit odd, but at least we could see that they were mushrooms. She led us to an aisle with big clear plastic bins and used the scoop to place steel-cut oats and quinoa in paper bags. Louisa explained to Genna that quinoa was once cultivated by the Incas in South America and that it was especially good for you because it had a lot of protein.

"I like to cook a batch on Sundays for the rest of the week," Louisa said. "Depending on what I have around, I might add in some feta cheese or some tomatoes. It's also really good with nuts and basil. Then, you can just eat a little at a time when you feel like having a snack."

"Yum, that sounds good," Genna said. "You have to admit, though, that it looks like birdseed too."

"A lot of my favorite foods do!" Louisa said with a satisfied laugh. We ventured to the aisle with Asian foods, and Louisa bought rice noodles for soup and jars of curry paste for stir-fry. "You know, Genna, the Steeping Leaf has always prided itself on offering its customers delectable cakes and sweets. I *don't* always eat birdseed . . . I eat treats, too. I use real butter. But I think as long as you have those wonderful things a little at a time, it's fine."

"That makes sense." Genna looked very thoughtful. I hoped that she'd take Louisa's example to heart . . . and maybe even educate her mom as well.

We were almost ready to go, but I hadn't chosen any ingredients yet for my next scone. I was completely out of ideas, just when I needed to impress dozens of new blog followers.

"I want to buy some new scone ingredients," I said, "but I don't know what to get. I want to make something healthy, but also so good that people will want to eat a half a dozen in one sitting."

"Well, let's start with whole wheat pastry flour," Louisa suggested. "That way, even if you put heavy cream in it, it'll at least have some fiber."

We headed for the baking aisle and Louisa added her favorite brand of whole wheat flour to the cart.

"I know that the competition knows the secret ingredient is tea," Genna said thoughtfully. "But they don't know what *kind* of tea, and they don't know what we're *doing* with it. What if we used brewed tea for the recipe instead of tea leaves, and soaked the fruit in it first. Like, currants soaked in a delicious black vanilla tea or something?"

"Wow. I *love* that idea." I grinned at Genna.

I zipped from aisle to aisle, picking out special ingredients for what was destined to become my masterpiece.

**Extra-Healthy Tea Smoothie**
This smoothie makes for a great breakfast or snack!

**Ingredients**
1 cup pomegranate-flavored black tea
⅓ cup organic whey (The acai-flavored whey from Tera's Whey in Reedsburg, WI, is awesome!)
½ cup blueberries
½ cup strawberries
1 banana

Add all ingredients to a blender. Blend on low for 1 minute. Then, increase the speed and blend on high for 1 minute. Makes 2 delicious smoothies.

July 30   4:31 p.m.

# Chapter Fourteen

Tea is the new tea.
—Unknown

H alt, Teashop Girl! Who is spying *now*, Annie Green?" The last voice I wanted to hear in the whole wide world shouted at me from the cereal aisle just as Louisa, Genna, and I pushed the cart toward the checkout.

Zach. *How* was this possible?

"Zach, do not come near this cart." I put myself between him and it, but it was too late. He left his friends behind and came bounding toward us.

"Mmm, white chocolate chips. I approve. When will the next scone be done? I'll take five." He saw everything we picked out, even though I was leaning over the cart and trying to stack the less interesting foods on top.

"Zach," Genna said. "Go away. Stop spying on superior life forms. We're trying to do something special here, and you're driving Annie crazy."

"He is not," I said. I stood up straight again, folded my arms over my chest, and glared at him. Okay, maybe a little crazy. But I wasn't going to admit it.

"Hello, young man," Louisa said. We all turned to her, unconsciously waiting for a verdict. Surely Louisa would understand why I wouldn't want a spy around the shop. Period. Especially a rude one who *kissed* me and then tried to pretend it didn't happen. "How is your family?"

All three of us gaped at her. Zach recovered right away, though, and said, "They're good."

"Tell your parents to come in and see us at the shop," Louisa said. "I'd like to share some new teas with them."

"Okay," Zach said. He didn't seem to know what to say after that, so he ambled back to his friends.

"Louisa," I hissed. "I think he's the one who messaged SweetCakes about our secret ingredient. We need to ban him! And his family," I added. "Immediately! And I need to buy all new scone ingredients. Let's put the currants and white chocolate back on the shelf."

"Nonsense, dear. Don't worry. It's time to check out."

Louisa gave me a squeeze and I made a face at Genna. She shrugged helplessly.

I loved my grandmother. But sometimes she didn't get it at *all*. I bet boys were a lot easier to deal with when she was young.

Genna and I helped Louisa put her groceries away, and then I went home and straight to bed. I wanted my next blog post to be extra special. I planned to hand out fliers promoting SteepingLeafScone.com at the farmer's market on Saturday, which meant that I'd need to be up early tomorrow for baking and taste testing.

When I woke up, I didn't go to the shop. Instead I planned to use our kitchen at home for my next scone. That way, no customers would be tempted to spy on me and I'd have more space. With the deadline fast approaching, I planned to make two different recipes. We were running out of time to find *the* scone.

## To Do: Friday, July 31

- Bake scones.
- Do an awesome and hopefully funny blog post about said scones.

- *Get fliers ready for the farmer's market.*
- *Help Zoe contact school-board members about cafeteria food. Like, yesterday (oops).*
- *Forget Zach was born.*
- *Figure out what to do about hair before high school starts and/or convince parents and Louisa to invest in central air.*

I was surprised to find my mom typing on her laptop at the kitchen table. It was Friday, and my parents were supposed to be at work. Usually the boys were either off skateboarding with their friends during the week or being supervised by their babysitter, a saintly neighbor.

"Hi, Mom, why are you here?" I asked.

"Good morning, sweetie. Luke is sick, so I'm working from home today."

"Oh." I was gone so much yesterday, I hardly even knew what was up with my own brothers. "What's wrong with him?"

"Probably just a cold, but he's feeling pretty bad. He's still sleeping."

"Is it okay if I make a scone recipe here today? I'm not going into the Leaf."

"Sure, hon. Just try to do it as quietly as possible. How come you don't want to bake with Louisa?"

"Oh, it's not that. It's just I'm worried someone at the Leaf is spying on my scones and giving secrets to the competition. I can be more secretive here at home," I explained. "Dad can eat them later."

"I see. Well, okay, then. Do we have the right ingredients?"

"I think so. I'm making a dummy scone today to throw people off the scent of my real, soon-to-hopefully-be-award-winning scone. So it doesn't really matter what I put in it, as long as it tastes good and the blog post looks nice."

"Sounds good."

My mom returned to her computer, and I pulled flour, sugar, and milk out and placed them on the counter. I decided to do something really unusual and pulled some precooked salad shrimp out of the freezer. I also grabbed some green onion from the crisper. My next scone would be a Rangoon Scone. I hoped it would work. I thawed the little shrimps in the sink and chopped up the green onion into tiny pieces. Next, I put all the ingredients together, added some salt, parsley, and garlic, and cut the dough into circles.

When the scones started to turn golden brown in the oven, I took some cream cheese out of the fridge. These scones would be served with a nice *schmear* of the stuff.

Just like the customers at the shop, my mom lifted her nose up as the aroma filled the kitchen.

"That smells unusual, Annie. What is it?"

"A shrimp scone," I said proudly.

"Well, goodness, I doubt that's ever been done before. I'll try one."

I plated a scone for my mom, and pulled it apart a little bit to spoon on some cream cheese. She smiled and took a bite.

"It's . . . interesting, dear."

Uh-oh. Chefs don't want to hear "interesting" when they serve up their latest creation. I plated one for myself, spread on the cream cheese, and took a nibble.

Lesson learned: Seafood does not mix with tea treats. FAIL.

"You know, I bet your father will like these," my mom said consolingly. "He eats anything. It's one of the reasons we get along so well," she added with a laugh.

"How come you don't like to cook?" I asked. My mom did cook sometimes, but I could always tell that she was in a rush and didn't really enjoy it.

"I don't know. Never have. I guess your grandmother is so good at it that I wanted to find my own thing instead of trying to match her. I always skipped the kitchen lessons in favor of practicing my instruments."

"Oh," was all I said. I wondered why daughters liked to be different from their mothers. I, for one, had never shown much interest in learning the flute.

"But I think it's wonderful that you're getting so good at it, honey," she said.

I looked at the shrimp scones and pulled a face. "You really think Dad will eat these?"

"Sure. And Billy. Just tell him you put something really gross in them. I always got him to eat his veggies when he was little by telling him they were covered in fresh worm sauce."

"EW!"

Later that day, I signed in to chat. I knew Zoe was spending most of her day trying to get somewhere with the school board, so she would probably be online.

> **cuppaAnnie:** hi zo
> **Kswiss211:** hi A, how come you're not at the Leaf? I went there before. I found this really great organization called REAP that I want us to join.
> **cuppaAnnie:** oh, sorry. I baked at home today to avoid the spy
> **Kswiss211:** oh. Louisa said some of the customers were asking about you
> **cuppaAnnie:** bunch o' spies. Which ones?
> **Kswiss211:** !
> **cuppaAnnie:** it could be anyone. how is it going?

**Kswiss211:** not well. Not one school-board member has answered my e-mails or called me back.
**cuppaAnnie:** oh

I was supposed to be helping her. I felt a twinge of guilt, but there was so much left to do to win the scone contest and I only had three weeks. I vowed to set aside some time during the weekend. I still needed to buy some school clothes too. And get a haircut. Argh!

**Kswiss211:** yeah. I'm really bummed out. Also, most of the people at my garden said they don't grow enough to donate to the schools.
**cuppaAnnie:** ☹
**Kswiss211:** so, I want to work with some farmer's market vendors instead. Can you come help me put together a video to send them? I want to film the difference between a gross school lunch and the kind I want them to serve
**cuppaAnnie:** that sounds neat. But I have to make a new scone yet today. My first one failed.
**Kswiss211:** oh. When will you be free?
**cuppaAnnie:** I don't know. I'll call you
**Kswiss211:** ☹

I logged off the computer. I felt bad, but what was I supposed to do? I didn't have that much more time left before the deadline. I hoped Zo wasn't too annoyed with me. I couldn't even think of a second scone to make anyway.

Dear readers,

Remember when I asked for extra-original recipe ideas? Well, I was totally serious about trying something outrageous, so I decided to make a scone unlike anyone's ever tasted before. Being daring in the kitchen is good, right?

Well, as it turns out, not always, especially when seafood is involved. I made an Asian-themed shrimp Rangoon scone, and I'm sorry to report it was a total fail. There is a reason people don't usually try to put shellfish in baked goods. Even serving it with cream cheese couldn't save it. My cat, dad, and brother liked my efforts, but I'm afraid a winning scone that does not make. ☺

Does anyone have any original ideas that don't attract all the neighborhood felines? Hehe.

Love, Annie

July 31  10:28 a.m.

## Chapter Fifteen

It's always tea-time.
—LEWIS CARROLL, *ALICE IN WONDERLAND*

After the "shrimp incident" I was bummed not to have a recipe to post. My mom reminded me that my blog didn't have to be all scones. I agreed and posted Zoe's quiche recipe. Then I spent some time posting nice comments on other people's blogs. I noticed SweetCakes wasn't just rude to me. Her (his?) particular brand of intimidating snark had found its way onto other blogs too. It seemed incredibly unfair that the SweetCakes blog continued to be in the top five on the leader board. I tried to remember what Louisa had said about just focusing on my own path, but it made me really mad. I also missed the Leaf, but I didn't want to go back there. Any one of the customers could be a spy.

## Possible Scone Spies

- Zach
- Oliver and Theresa ("Just moved here"? How convenient)
- That one lady at the shop who comes in and never smiles
- A barista from Corporate Coffee across the street
- ~~Tim~~ (Nah. Too busy)
- Zach

Fortunately, it was Saturday morning, and that meant one thing: farmer's market! I got my tote ready with a bottle of iced tea and hundreds of fliers for our blog. I wasn't going to shop today; I was just going down to promote SteepingLeafScone.com. Of course, a pumpkin bar for breakfast wouldn't hurt. Even if Zoe, Genna, and now Louisa were on major healthy-eating kicks, I wasn't about to give up my beloved Murphy Farms pumpkin bars.

I put on a yellow visor, then decided to leave it at home. The sky was actually a bit overcast and it was cooler than it had been. I tried to IM Zoe, just to make sure she wasn't really mad at me, but she didn't respond. She was starting to look ahead to the fall tennis season and that meant more hours on the court, so I just figured she wasn't at home. Genna was going shopping in Milwaukee with her mom, so I'd have to try to see her later.

I wondered if Zach would be at the market. For a split second I even hoped so. I missed him, even though I'd never admit it, not even to the Teashop Girls. Oh well. Things were better this way. I couldn't have anyone dripping lake water on my pretty fliers.

I skipped down the stairs. My whole family was at the table, minus Luke. My mom handed me a plate of scrambled eggs sprinkled with shredded cheddar.

"I'm serious, Dad," Billy said. "Why hasn't anyone invented it?"

"Invented what?" I asked.

"A sheet you put in the freezer before bed," my brother said excitedly. "You know, to stay cool when you're trying to sleep. You would pull it out and sleep on it and you wouldn't need air-conditioning. It would have a squishy layer of frozen water inside."

"Ew," Beth said.

"That's kind of not a bad idea," I said. "I'd use that." It was always so hard to fall asleep in the middle of summer when it was hot and sticky.

"What about condensation?" my dad asked, always the

engineer. "When the frozen sheet melted, you'd get the mattress all wet."

"Huh," Billy said. "I dunno."

I sat down at the table and noticed my dad was eating my gross scones.

"Dad, you don't have to eat those," I said.

"I think they're delicious," he replied, and took a giant bite. "See? I made an egg sandwich with mine."

He had. It looked pretty bad.

"Me too!" Billy pointed out. His own scone was basically a pile of crumbles on his plate. He was using his fingers to eat it, and not having a lot of success. A constant cascade of crumbs fell to the floor on all sides of my brother.

"Ugh," was all I could say. "Sorry, Mom."

"How about 'Sorry, Beth'?" my sister piped up. "They put them in the *microwave*, and now this whole place smells like cat food." So much for Beth being nicer than usual.

"No it doesn't, honey," my mom said. But she did pull the kitchen window open a little wider. "Eat your eggs."

"How's Luke?" I asked, choosing to ignore my sister's complaining.

"Being a baby," Billy said as he continued to spill his breakfast to Molly. Our dog was clearly in the shrimp-scone-fan category. The cats were circling pretty close too. Too bad they couldn't follow my blog.

"Billy! Don't you remember the last time you were sick and he stayed home and watched movies with you?" my dad reminded him.

"That's just because he had nothing better to do," Billy replied. "Mom! Don't give me all of his chores! No fair!"

My mom was at the dreaded white board. I saw that after I handed out my fliers downtown, I would have to sweep the front porch and water the garden and all the potted plants. Not bad.

"Okay, I'm going to the square," I announced as I finished my eggs. I rinsed my plate in the sink and put it in the dishwasher.

"Bye, Annie," my family called after me. "Have fun!"

I hopped on my bike and took the bike path toward the capitol square. It was peaceful since it was still early, and all the college students were away for the summer. I knew some people preferred Madison when the students were gone, but I missed them. The students made the city feel alive. I hoped to take my place among them when it was time. But I'd live in a dorm, of course, and not at home! Even if I went to Edgewater instead of UW, and that was about eight blocks from my house.

I locked up my bike near the central library and decided to stand on the west side of the capitol in a shaded spot. It felt a little odd to be alone. I was usually with either

Genna, Zoe, Louisa and the shop customers, or one of my family members. But it felt kind of good. I could walk anywhere on a whim. I bought my pumpkin bar, ate it, and began handing out my blog fliers. Most people just took them without looking at them, which was kind of disheartening. I should've brought free samples, like we had done with the tea at school in the spring.

I decided it might help to stand at a different part of the market loop, so I walked through the capitol building to the east side of the square. Even though I'd been in the state capitol a million times, it still made me catch my breath. The air inside was cool and still. All the marble and gold leaf made it look like a palace or a cathedral. I loved it.

On the other side of the square, I chose a spot not far from a restaurant called L'Etoile. There was a nearby café with wonderful baked goods called Batch Bakehouse, and I figured that anyone going in there might be interested in my contest. It had just opened a month earlier, but there was already a line down the block on both Saturday and Sunday. I handed out lots of fliers and got bolder about chatting with people to explain what I was doing. Several people offered encouragement and promised they'd check out the website when they got home. A few even went to it immediately on their phones and showed me when they hit the button to follow.

After about a half hour a tall man came out of the café

and walked over to me. He had short cropped hair and a flour-covered apron. I felt nervous; he looked very businesslike. I thought I might have annoyed him by chatting up his customers about the things *I* was baking instead of the things he was baking. Oops.

"Are you the scone girl from the Steeping Leaf?" he asked.

"Um, yes. I'm Annie Green." I shifted my bag to my shoulder and put out my hand to shake his.

He shook it. "I'm Tom Hines, the baker here. One of my customers told me about your contest. You know, you're not allowed to hand out fliers down here without a permit."

"I'm not?" I blushed. I didn't know that.

"No. I'm surprised a police officer didn't stop you."

"I'm sorry."

"Hey, it doesn't bother me. So, what do they say?" He reached for one of my fliers and I handed it over. I put the rest away. It wouldn't help my cause if I got arrested. Thank goodness I looked young for my age. That's probably why the fuzz hadn't paid attention to me.

"I have less than a month to qualify for the finals in Chicago," I explained. "I have to get as many blog followers as possible before then, so I came out to the market to introduce myself." I still felt scared, talking to a real professional, but fortunately, my time as a barista had made me more confident. Still, I couldn't tell yet if he wanted to help me or get me to go away.

"What have you baked so far?" he asked.

"Well, I'm experimenting with both savory and sweet," I replied, warming up. "But my latest effort was a complete disaster. I was trying to be original, but it turns out shrimp does not go with scones."

He chuckled. "That is original, I'll agree with you there."

"I did make a really good bacon tomato one, though. And a delicious cookies and cream variety. I'm still working on one perfect recipe to bake if I make it to the finals. One perfect *secret* recipe."

"I see. Well, would you care to come in early some morning and help out? I'd be happy to show you a few tricks of the trade."

It seemed that I had been sized up, and that I'd passed. I grinned. "I'd love that. When?"

"How about Tuesday. Be here at four a.m."

"Wow. Okay!"

I shook his hand again and skipped away toward State Street.

I had a good feeling about this.

# Steeping Leaf Scone.com

I've got another special treat for you, readers! Zoe has created the best quiche recipe ever. You've got to make it, try it, and love it. ☺

**Zoe's Veggie Quiche Recipe**

**Ingredients**

1 frozen pie crust, thawed
½ pound grated cheddar cheese
½ cup grape tomatoes, cut in half
½ cup fresh mushrooms, cleaned and diced
¼ cup sun-dried tomatoes, soaked and diced
1 tablespoon white onion, diced
4 large eggs
¾ cup half-and-half
1 teaspoon chopped fresh basil
1 teaspoon salt
½ teaspoon black pepper

Preheat oven to 375 degrees Fahrenheit. Thaw the frozen pie crust and place it in a glass pie pan. Place the cheese on the pie crust first. Place the grape tomatoes, mushrooms, sun-dried tomatoes, and white onion on the pie crust and spread them around evenly. In a medium-size bowl, mix the eggs, half-and-half, basil, salt, and pepper together. Add the egg mixture to the pie pan slowly. Some of the vegetables inside will float; that's fine. Place in the oven and bake for approximately 40 to 45 minutes or until the center is solid and the blade of a paring knife comes out free of clear liquid when inserted in the center. Cool slightly and serve warm. Makes 8 servings.

August 1  8:17 a.m.

## Chapter Sixteen

Tea . . . is a religion of the art of life.
—OKAKURA

**SCONE CONTEST LEADER BOARD**

1. Master Baker.............587 followers
2. Scone-y Nation.........572 followers
3. PastrySwagger..........494 followers
4. SweetCakes.............431 followers
5. Miss Cuppycake........404 followers

11. SteepingLeafScone....145 followers

Have you ever set your alarm for three thirty a.m.? I bet you haven't, especially not in the middle of summer. Unless your parents wanted to take you on a trip and your plane was going to leave at five. Then it wouldn't seem so crazy. Anyway, that's what I did on Monday night, the evening before I was to learn how to bake from a real pro. I felt excited, but also sure I wouldn't get much sleep at all. I promised myself that I would take good notes, so even if I was too tired to remember anything I learned, I'd at least have something to show for it.

My mom was veeeeery reluctant to let me go bake in the middle of the night with a stranger, but fortunately, she called Louisa. It turns out that my grandmother knew Tom Hines and had even helped him pick out which teas to serve in his café when it opened. Thank goodness Madison was such a relatively small town and that Louisa knew practically everyone who'd ever lived on the isthmus. My dad didn't want me to bike in the middle of the night, so he agreed to drive me downtown and then just go to work early. Once in a while I have to admit it: My parents are pretty great.

When I arrived at the bakery and peered through the front door, Tom was already there, along with another person I'd never met. She had short hair dyed pink and a ring in her eyebrow. I knocked and then put my Steeping Leaf apron on. I was tying it while trying not to drop my notebook and pen when the door swung open.

"Good morning!" Tom bellowed. I winced and blinked, trying to wake up.

"Good morning," I said, considerably quieter.

"I'm impressed you showed up," he said. "Looks like we have a real baker here, Priscilla. This is Priscilla, she is my assistant. This is Annie."

"Hey," was all she said. It looked like she was preparing a work space, arranging various ingredients on a large woodblock table. It was okay with me that she wasn't very talkative. I didn't feel super chatty myself. Even my hair was less poofy than usual at this hour.

"We're going to make croissants first," Tom announced. "You know what the most important ingredient is when you're making a croissant?"

I thought about some of the best ones I'd tried. They were always deliciously flaky and extra buttery.

"Butter?" I answered hesitantly.

"Bingo!" he cried. "You have the soul of a gourmand, my young friend."

I couldn't be sure, but I thought I saw Priscilla roll her eyes a little bit. I smiled.

"Thank you." I made a note.

"Oh, you don't need to take notes, kiddo. We're just talking. If you want to win this thing, you have to *become* a baker through and through, not follow notes."

"Okay," I said. No wonder Louisa had encouraged my mom to let me hang out here. This Tom character was cut from the same cloth as my Zen grandmother. "How do I do that?"

"Take a deep breath," he instructed. I did what he said. The shop smelled good, like butter and chocolate. "Deeper!" I tried again, this time with my eyes closed.

"Good. A real baker lives and breathes her work." Tom sat his wide frame down on a small stool and reached for a stick of butter. I could already see that the bulk of the real baking would be done by Priscilla. She worked efficiently as her boss gestured to another stool for me to sit.

"Thank you," I said. I didn't try to take a note. I set my notebook on the floor, in fact.

"First, we're going to talk ingredients. This here is the finest butter in the state. It comes directly from a farmer in Dodge County. We've been friends since we were both in diapers."

"Wow."

"Exactly," Tom said. "It's *very* important to know precisely where everything comes from. I know what the cows eat, even. Now, what do you plan to put into your winning scone?" he asked.

"Well, I'm not quite sure yet. I know that my secret ingredient will be tea—even though it's not technically a secret anymore—and I was thinking of using currants or blackberries and small toffee pieces."

"Sounds good. But might I suggest that you don't need any of that?"

"I don't?"

"Nope. If you did it right, you could easily win this contest with a plain scone using only the most basic ingredients: flour, buttermilk, baking soda, egg, and a pinch of salt. Maybe a little butter."

"That seems . . . hard to believe," I finally said. I mean, I actually loved plain scones more than most people did, because they were delicious with clotted cream and a little jam. But this was the big time. A trip to *London* was on the line. I was pretty sure I needed to bring as much razzle-dazzle to the stage in Chicago as was humanly possible. Assuming I made it that far, of course.

"It's perfectly reasonable to believe. A baker lives and dies by these basic ingredients. If each one of them is of the highest quality and integrity, it doesn't matter what frills you add.

"It's like with people," he continued, leaning back on his stool. Priscilla was *definitely* rolling her eyes now. But she also winked at me. "Say you have a person who always has the most be-yoo-tiful clothing. Tell me, would you like that person with the pretty clothes, if she were rude? No, you wouldn't. Or take a person who happened to be an incredibly famous singer. Would you want to spend time with him if he were dishonest? I should hope not. The fashion sense and the singing talent in a person are like berries and toffee in a scone: a bonus. But what you have to have, what you *must* have, is character. And the character of your scone will come from the flour, the buttermilk, and the butter . . . and from how you handle these cornerstones. As for the character of a human being? That, I cannot help you with. But fortunately, you don't have to bake one of those." He cracked up. And, I'm not even kidding, slapped his knee a few times. I grinned.

"I'm glad I came here, Mr. Hines. This is all really interesting."

"You're grandmother is a good baker too," Tom said. "She loves food. And that's the first thing you've got to do."

"I love food too. Especially with tea."

"Good. Now all you need is some practice. Bake your scone again and again until the proportion of ingredients to each other is exactly right. Practice until you could make them with your eyes closed. Then—and only then—think about what your bonus ingredients will be. But trust me. You don't need 'em."

"Got it. So how can I help here today?"

We got serious about baking then. Priscilla showed me how to handle the delicate croissant dough, and Tom continued to share his baking philosophy—really his philosophy about everything—with me. He thought it was important for bakers to be happy people, because he felt the emotions of the person making the food could be tasted by his customers. He also believed in sharing and trading ingredients, because that way, the goodwill of lots of people went into a single loaf of bread. Finally, he thought the best way to make truly delicious food was to make it for people that you care about.

"You know what the secret ingredient in all of *my* bread is, Annie?"

I wasn't sure, so I said, "Butter?" again.

He chuckled. "Close, my new friend. Joy."

# SteepingLeafScone.com

Dear readers,

I had the honor of baking with a true Madison original this morning, Mr. Tom Hines. He taught me the importance of using high-quality ingredients in my scones and how to bake with joy. Before I forget, I wanted to share some of his life philosophies with you. Then, I need more sleep! Bakers get up EARLY.

**Q: Which chefs or bakers inspire you?**
**Tom:** Julia Child, of course. If you haven't read *My Life in France*, her memoir, you must. She was filled with *joie de vivre* and a pure love of food, people, and experiences. She's my hero, truly. Julia liked to say, "You don't have to cook fancy or complicated masterpieces—just good food from fresh ingredients." I completely agree.

**Q: Where do you get your ingredients?**
**Tom:** Directly from farmers whenever possible. Sometimes I visit the farms in person; other times I go to farmer's markets. I understand that people love the convenience of large grocery stores, but in my humble opinion, smaller is better. Getting to know my local food producers, butchers, coffee roasters, and gardeners is fun.

**Q: Coffee or tea?**
**Tom:** Coffee.

**Q: What??**
**Tom:** Sorry.

Q: Any advice for new bakers?
**Tom:** Don't be afraid to get creative. Don't be afraid of any part of it, really. Try everything, learn from your mistakes, do it again. Food is life, and life is supposed to be messy. If you're clean all the time, you're not trying hard enough. I want to see flour in your hair, people!

Q: **Thank you. Even though you like coffee better than tea, I still think you're cool.**
**Tom:** I'm honored, Annie Green. Knock 'em dead.
I'll certainly try, Mr. Hines!

<3 Annie

August 4  9:03 a.m.

## Chapter Seventeen

I am so fond of tea that I could write a whole dissertation on
its virtues.
—JAMES BOSWELL

M y time with Tom Hines made a big
impression on me. After I went home
at nine a.m. to take a nap, I couldn't fall
asleep right away. I kept thinking about what Tom had
said about the basic ingredients of the scone and how
they compared to the basic ingredients of a person. I was
lucky to know people with so many great flavors: Zoe
with her tennis talents and gardening skills, Genna with
her artistic ability and outgoing nature, Louisa with her
warmth and knowledge of tea and yoga and healthy food.
But then I thought about how, according to Tom, all of
that stuff was just a bonus. What really mattered was that

they were all good people. Genna, Zoe, and Louisa were *kind*. They were loyal. They were honest, and they cared.

My mind leaped to Zach. What ingredients was *he* made of? If you had asked me six months ago, I would have said that he was made of all rotten things and, like, gum wrappers. Energy drinks. Saliva. Then, around the beginning of summer, I'd begun to change my mind. It seemed like he was made of mostly good ingredients, with a few snotty ones that still needed to be picked out and discarded. Or ignored.

Now? I had no idea, but I was tempted to return to my original assessment. It was all so confusing. Since I couldn't fall asleep, I turned on the computer and checked all of the leader blogs. Master Baker had just posted an all-organic scone recipe that was getting a lot of comments. I made a note to myself to look for organic ingredients the next time I went shopping. SweetCakes had a very complicated recipe for biscotti posted. I was glad the contest was scones and not biscotti . . . that had to be baked twice! I saw that she didn't have many comments at all. Unfortunately, she *did* have a lot of followers.

**Zmoney:** Attention Teashop Girl . . . your system has been breached by a double agent.
**cuppaAnnie:** ZACH! So you admit it. Spy.

I hadn't realized my chat dot was green. The smart thing to do would've been to sign off. But I didn't want to.

> **Zmoney:** I admit nothing.
> **cuppaAnnie:** What do you want, Zach?
> **Zmoney:** I am at the Leaf right now, contaminating your ingredients. Just so you know.
> **cuppaAnnie:** !!! Stop it!
> **Zmoney:** LOL

I buckled my sandals. I had to go make sure everything was okay at the Leaf. It was one thing if Zach wanted to hang around and bother me . . . but I couldn't have him pestering Louisa or getting into my stuff!

> **cuppaAnnie:** Are you there or not?
> **Zmoney:** Not.
> **cuppaAnnie:** Fine. Can I ask you a question?
> **Zmoney:** No.
> **cuppaAnnie:** Why did you kiss me?

I held my breath. I'd wanted to ask him ever since it happened. But there was no way I could do it in person. It would be too weird. And besides, he'd probably just pretend he had no idea what I was talking about. Online, maybe we could have a real conversation. Maybe.

**Zmoney:** I have to go.

I stared at the computer screen, dismayed. Of course he had to go. His dot turned gray. I frowned and went back to reading scone blogs. There were so many helpful comments from readers. Maybe my readers could help too. I decided to post a poll to see what everyone's favorite scone was so far.

After I finished my poll I was about to log off when I noticed Zach's chat dot was green again. I know this is silly, but I wanted to talk to him, so I tried a different tack.

> **cuppaAnnie:** My brother is trying to invent a sheet you put in the freezer.
> **Zmoney:** Why?
> **cuppaAnnie:** To stay cool while you're sleeping.
> **Zmoney:** Huh. That could work. If you used the same gel stuff they make ice packs out of. But if the layer of gel was too thin, it wouldn't work, and if it was too thick, the thing would be too big for the freezer.

I smiled. Nothing like nerd talk to get Zach perked up. I wasn't sure how to go from talking about weird inventions to asking if he planned to try to kiss me again, though. It turns out that talking isn't really easier online after all.

> **cuppaAnnie:** Yeah.
> **Zmoney:** You know what else they should make sheets out of? Bubble wrap.
> **cuppaAnnie:** Why?
> **Zmoney:** It would be comfortable. And if you couldn't sleep, you could pop it.
> **cuppaAnnie:** I guess.
> **Zmoney:** Don't pretend you don't love popping bubble wrap. And pimples!
> **cuppaAnnie:** gross, Zach.
> **Zmoney:** Wanna see something really gross? Search for "boil lancing" on YouTube.
> **cuppaAnnie:** UGGGG. WHY DO I EVER TALK TO YOU?
> **Zmoney:** What?

I rolled my eyes at the computer and signed off. Having a conversation with Zach was even more frustrating than trying to talk my parents into getting me a cell phone. I decided to forget about him for a while and get back to what really mattered.

I considered Tom's secret to making good bread. I certainly hadn't felt much joy lately when I made my scones. I was so worried about SweetCakes and a spy at the Leaf that I didn't want to share my creations with our customers. I didn't even want to be around them, and usually the Leaf was my favorite spot on earth. Also, I was so focused on winning that I wasn't making any time for Zoe or *her* quest. In fact, I hadn't seen her in days. I tried to call her. Instead of reaching her, I heard "This is Zoe. Please leave me a message and I will call you back!" I took off my sandals and fell into a fitful sleep and dreamed about the contest. I kept trying to bake without any ingredients at all.

# SteepingLeafScone.com

Dear readers,

I'm conducting a poll to find out which of my scones you like the best (or would like to try the most). Please vote!

**Parmesan Berry**

☐☐☐☐☐☐☐ 7

**Chocolate Chip**

☐☐☐ 3

# SteepingLeafScone.com

**Bacon**

▯▯▯▯▯▯▯▯▯ 9

**Cookies & Cream**

▯▯▯▯ 4

Total Votes: 23

Days Left for Voting: 14

August 4  9:26 a.m.

# Chapter Eighteen

Teapot is on, the cups are waiting. Favorite chairs anticipating. No matter what I have to do, my friend there's always time for you.
—UNKNOWN

As soon as I woke up from my nap, I raced over to Zoe's house. She wasn't there, so I went home, got my bike out of the garage, and headed to her garden plot. As I pedaled, I thought about what I wanted to say. I felt I owed Zoe an apology. All summer she had been generously sharing her food and her time with me, coming into the Leaf almost every day. And when she had needed *my* help, I hadn't made the time. Zoe was always so even, so easy to get along with. She would never make a fuss . . . but she shouldn't have to. Zoe wasn't there, either, so I tried the tennis court in Vilas Park. Finally, I spotted her. She was alone, practicing her serve. *Whack! Whack!* Her serve was dangerous.

I didn't walk into the court; I just went up to the fence behind her. When she took a break to go collect balls in the hopper, I spoke up.

"Zo?"

"Annie? Hey." There was coolness in her voice.

"Hey. Listen, I'm sorry I didn't make time to help you earlier. With the school board and the farmer's market people. I've been so obsessed with scones that I kind of forgot there's other stuff going on."

She bounced a ball between her racket and the ground, hard. "Yeah."

I could tell Zoe wanted to say something else, so I just waited for a minute. It was important not to interrupt her when she looked this serious.

"It's like it's always about *you* sometimes," she finally said. "I know the Leaf and the Teashop Girls are important. But once in a while Genna and I are going to want to do stuff that has nothing to do with tea. And I want you to care about it." Zoe's words hurt. I'd accused Genna of the very same crime—being self-absorbed—when she'd decided to go to theater camp. It occurred to me that being a good friend was not something that could be done by accident. You had to work at it, and pay attention.

"I do care. A lot. I'm totally taking the rest of the day off from scones. I need to start all over anyway, but that can wait. Can I help you today?" I hoped it wasn't too late to make it up to my friend. I knew that sometimes I got a little overfocused on what was happening in my own life. I remembered my mom and dad poking fun at Beth when we were younger for being a self-obsessed teenager. I guess I wasn't any better.

Zoe smiled and smoothed her hair, refastening a barrette. One of her best qualities was that she never, ever stayed mad. "Okay. See, what I want to do is make a short, like, public service announcement about the community garden. I want it to show people what we could do for the schools if only we could partner up. Hopefully it'll turn out really cool. My stepdad says we can borrow his digital camera. We could even put it on your food blog if you wanted. I thought I'd put together some sample lunches, show them on camera, and flash some basic nutrition information. I want to film right at the farmer's market, and at the school, but we can start with a short segment at the Leaf. . . ."

Zoe kept talking a mile a minute.

"Augh!" Okay, slow down. I need to make some notes!" I laughed.

"That's a good idea. I get kind of excited," she agreed, scooping up a tennis ball with the outside edge of her shoe and her racket. I collected a couple, too, and tossed them to her.

"Let's go to the Leaf," I suggested. "I need some tea to keep up with you."

Zoe giggled and agreed.

The shop was busy when we arrived, but Louisa seemed to have it under control. She sat at a table with two little girls and an older lady wearing a lovely hat. Louisa was showing the girls how to stir their tea without clanking the spoon against the sides of the cup.

"See, like this," Louisa said, carefully moving a small spoon in her cup. "Very gentle. There's no rush. Now you try."

The girls imitated Louisa. One accidentally clinked her cup. "Oops!"

Louisa giggled in delight. "It's okay, sweetheart. You know what the most important rule of tea is?"

"What?" the girls asked.

My grandmother met my eyes and I smiled. "Annie here, one of the *original* Teashop Girls, can tell you."

"The most important rule of tea is to enjoy yourself!" I exclaimed. "Tea is the best time of day." I made sure both girls had pink Teashop Girls buttons and got punch cards for them as well. I mentioned that they had to come back for birthday tea to get a free pot.

I explained to Louisa what Zoe wanted to do, and she said it sounded lovely.

"You can use the counter or the last free table on the patio, my dearheart."

"I've also decided not to bake at home again," I announced. "All the rest of my scones will be created here. For our customers."

"Why the change of heart, sugarpie?" Louisa asked. "And what kind of tea would you like today?"

"Mr. Hines taught me there's more to a good scone than the flour and the sugar. I was wrong not to include our customers. I need them . . . and their taste buds. I'm going to practice making all plain scones next week, so the spy will get bored anyway. I'll take some oolong."

"Sounds like you're on the right track, my lovely. Jasmine or plain?"

"Plain. Thank you. I'm going back to basics, Louisa."

She smiled. "Does that mean no more bacon?"

"I'll never say no to bacon, but I'm just not putting it in the batter for now. I want to get really good at making a basic recipe," I explained. "The scone has to be delectable without all the extras."

"That's funny . . . what you're saying reminds me of how I feel about tea," Louisa said.

"It does?"

"Sure. See, we have all these fancy cups and pots and varieties . . ." My grandmother gestured to the Leaf's shelves, which were stocked with a lifetime's collection of tea things. Her wrist was decorated with a funky charm bracelet and draped with the end of her sheer aquamarine scarf. I loved all of the pots and cups, and I knew Louisa did too. "But really, all we need are the tea leaves, some hot water in a pot, and one good friend to share it with. The rest is just frills."

"I heart the frills," I said. But I knew what she meant. I supposed the hard part was to remember to be grateful for them but not too terribly attached. That way, the simple things in life could make you happy and you didn't have to spend every minute chasing extra stuff.

Zoe arrived carrying two huge bags of food. Genna was right behind her with a big light, the camera, and a tote with beauty supplies.

"Hey, I called Gen, too. She said she's going to do my makeup for the shoot." Zoe crossed her eyes at Louisa and me. I giggled.

"Hello, girls," Louisa greeted my friends. "Who's having tea? I'm making some oolong for Annie." They both gave her a hug.

"I'll have peppermint!" Zoe said.

"Ooh, good choice, dear." Louisa nodded. "Mint is so cooling on a hot day. And for you, lovely Genna?"

"I'll take jasmine pearl," Gen said, tapping her finger

to her mouth thoughtfully. "I feel like something flowery. I like your scarf, Louisa."

"Why, thank you! Annie's mother bought it for me." Louisa rearranged the sheer fabric. I blinked at her, surprised to hear my mom had such good taste.

"She did? When?" I asked.

"Hmm . . . a long time ago. I want to say at some sort of music educators' conference in Savannah? It's one of my favorites."

Genna and Zoe surveyed the Leaf and chose a table to set up at. Zoe wanted to use the counter.

Sure enough, once Zoe set out the two sample school lunches she'd made—a turkey wrap and a pasta salad made with whole wheat pasta, vegetables from her garden, and feta cheese—and photos of some less healthy lunches for comparison—pizza and chicken nuggets—Genna got to work powdering Zo's nose.

"I'm only agreeing to this because you said the lights would make me look shiny," Zoe said to Genna.

"Trust the professional," Gen replied. "Here, wear this scarf." She took off the bright blue scarf she had looped around her neck and put it around Zoe's. It looked really pretty against Zo's smooth black hair and white shirt. Then, to Louisa, Genna said, "I made wheat berries for lunch. I put them in my salad. My mom liked them."

"Wonderful, dear. You look very well." Louisa prepared a pot of tea for Gen and one for Zo. Genna blushed and said, "Thank you."

"How is my hair?" Zoe asked. Her shiny black hair looked amazing, as usual. Genna pulled a bobby pin out of her own hair and used it to pin back Zo's. It looked pretty.

"Perfect."

"Annie?" Zoe asked. "Will you do the camera? When I point to something like one of these photos, you'll have to zoom in. Let's practice first."

"Yes. Okay, good idea." I felt honored that Zoe wanted me to be the cameraperson. She handed me the camera and explained how to zoom. We ran through Zoe's short presentation. She started by introducing herself. "I'm Zoe Malik, and I'll be a freshman this year at Madison West." Then she talked about the work that she and other local gardeners had been doing all summer. She said that though they were proud to give some of their produce to local food banks, they wanted to do more. I held the camera steady and kept it focused on her face. As she gestured to the food, I slowly panned over to it.

"The foods you see here were all prepared using ingredients grown almost all in Madison. With simple choices like these, we can cut back on the amount of salt and sugar we're eating." I zoomed in on the food as Zoe gave some basic nutrition information. When she compared it with the food in the photos, the difference was huge. There was so much more salt in the processed foods than there was in the wrap or in the pasta salad.

Zoe concluded her presentation by looking right into the camera.

"Please let local farmer's market vendors sell their produce to the schools each week. Use the fresh fruits and vegetables as quickly as possible, or freeze them for the winter. Madison kids deserve healthy food! Thank you."

It was great. Zoe came across as so knowledgeable and sincere. I couldn't imagine anyone in a position of authority saying no. Sure, it might be a bit complicated to get school lunch food from multiple sources. But who could really say that those chicken nuggets looked appetizing when they saw the alternative?

Both Genna and I hugged Zoe.

"Yeah, I think that was pretty good." Zoe grinned. "I can add some graphics later. Let's do it again. I'll film at the garden tomorrow."

"Don't forget to vary your volume a little bit as you're speaking. You know, a bit like a newscaster?" Genna suggested. "People pay closer attention when tone is dynamic," she added sagely.

"And breathe, sweetheart," Louisa added. "The first take was ever-so-slightly rushed. But wonderful."

When we had a few great takes, Genna said, "That's a wrap."

"Yes, it is. A turkey one. Let's eat." Zoe grinned.

Genna groaned but took a bite. "How's the scone leader board looking today, Annie?"

"I'm not checking it today," I replied. "But I'm sure once I put Zoe's video on my blog, I'll shoot up into at least eighth or ninth."

"Totally."

# SteepingLeafScone.com

Dear readers,

My BFF Zoe has been working to let people know more about healthy local food options. She's hoping to get fresh Wisconsin produce into the schools. I'm so proud of Zo's hard work. We made a terrific video about it that I'll post soon.

In the meantime enjoy this pic from Zoe's recent trip to the farmer's market. Yay, plums!

Love, Annie

August 4 8:40 p.m.

## Chapter Nineteen

"Tea and water give each other life," the Professor was saying. "The tea is still alive. This tea has tea and water vitality," he added. ". . . Afterwards, the taste still happens . . . It rises like velvet . . . It is a performance."

—JASON GOODWIN, *THE GUNPOWDER GARDENS*

The next day, I baked a plain scone at the Leaf. First, I asked Louisa about the best places to get each individual ingredient. We talked butter, and I learned that there are actually awards given out to butter makers every year. She told me about Lurpak, a Danish butter that is very light and creamy. I got some at the store and it was delicious. I felt like a bit of a traitor to my dairy state, but it seemed even Wisconsin cheese makers were enamored with the stuff, so it had to be special.

Next up: eggs. I already knew from Zoe that getting eggs from free-range chickens is best, and it's even better if you can get eggs that have just been laid that same day.

It turns out—you'll *never* believe this—that Mr. Arun, my former principal and Louisa's current amor, has a chicken coop in *his own backyard* on the near east side. With one phone call Louisa promised that fresh eggs would arrive in a half hour.

After doing some research online, I settled on King Arthur white all-purpose flour. I went to the co-op on my bike for some fresh organic buttermilk. I was ready to bake!

I began by putting on some upbeat music—Louisa's old Van Morrison *Moondance* record—and cleared my mind. I prepared some premium matcha from AOI Tea, my current favorite tea, and got busy. Just as I had pulled out every bowl I would need, Mr. Arun arrived with the eggs. They were tan in color and just a tad warm, which seemed odd. I knew it meant they were extremely fresh.

"Thank you so much!" I exclaimed. "These are perfect. I'll use one now and the rest tomorrow, Mr. A." I put them away. "Would you like some tea?"

"I would. How about a pot of chai, Annie?" He sat on a stool at the counter.

"You got it. Louisa was just chatting with a delivery person in back. She'll be right out." I scooped a generous portion of chai tea into one of our green single-serving pots and added hot water. I handed it to Mr. Arun with a cup and some cream. "This tea needs to steep for three minutes," I explained, giving him a little sand timer. We needed to order more of those; they were a big hit with the little Teashop Girls.

"And not a moment less." He winked, turning it over.

I knew he was teasing me a bit, but I didn't mind. "You can't rush good tea, Mr. A."

"Are you ready for high school?" my principal—I mean *former* principal—asked.

"Not really. Can you call West for me and mention that I'm a great student and should get straight A's?" I asked with a grin. Hey, it didn't hurt to try.

"I'll think about it." He smiled back. "As long as you keep up with your homework, you'll be just fine." Mr. Arun was an educator, through and through. Even in the middle of summer. Louisa emerged from the back just then.

"Hello, handsome," she said. They smooched, and I blushed for them. I'd get used to it eventually, but not today. "Ah, chai. Smells nice. May I have a cup, Annie love?" Louisa joined us at the counter, and I fetched a cup for her that matched his. I mixed my scones and popped them into the oven.

A half hour later, we shared some truly delicious scones. Mr. Arun, Louisa, and I tried the first three. Though the scones were plain, they were incredibly pleasant to eat. They had turned out very moist and delicious. I loved the way the jam snuck into the nooks and crannies when we spooned it on.

"Exquisite," Mr. Arun raved.

"Delightful," Louisa added, careful to swallow before she spoke. I grinned.

I handed out every last one of them with jam and clotted cream.

"Annie, these are . . . so incredibly amazing," Theresa said with her mouth still full. "Pardon me. Yum."

"They're almost creamy. And moist," Oliver observed. "They don't even crumble."

I smiled with pleasure. Was it possible that I'd actually take a *plain* scone to the finals if I made it? I couldn't decide. I remembered what Tom had said about practice and vowed to make the same recipe the next day . . . hopefully without even looking at the recipe.

I took close-up photos of the scones and of the ingredients I had used. I did a detailed blog post about my new scone. It turned out well. I'd forgotten how pretty white clotted cream and red jam looked against a simple scone. I used a blue plate for the shot and it really popped.

I cleaned everything up, did my dishes, and visited each table to see if anyone needed hot water. Ling had broken up the scone sample on Hieu's stroller tray, and he was actually eating it instead of flinging it around. "Amazing," she said. "I think he loves it, Annie. Good job!"

"Scone!" I looked at Hieu in surprise. I'd never heard him say it before.

"What was that, little buddy? You like the scone?"

"Scone!" he repeated.

"That's the first time I've heard him say that," Ling said, pleased. "Cute. Can you say 'Annie,' Hieu?"

"Scone!" We laughed. When I went back to check the blog, I saw two new developments. First, SteepingLeafScone. com was in tenth place on the leader board. Yes!

And second, SweetCakes was back.

**SweetCakes:** Plain? Really, Steeping Leaf? Really? It's like you're not even trying. Pathetic.

I turned off the computer. But not before sticking out my tongue at it.

I wanted to make sure that Zoe knew I cared about her goal of getting local, healthy food into the schools, so I went to find her at the garden. She was pulling grape tomatoes off the vine and grinned when she saw me.

"Hey!"

"Hey," I said. "Need any help?"

"Sure." She tossed me some gloves. The grape tomato plants dominated about a quarter of Zoe's plot, so there were a lot of them to pick.

"What's happening with the video?"

"Well, not too much. A couple of school administrators sent e-mails saying they like it, but it's really complicated, and a lot of people are already working on the issue."

"Complicated how?"

"Well, there's only one central kitchen in Madison for all the schools. Everything is shipped from there, and heated on-site. It would be hard for one local farmer to come up with, like, three thousand pounds of carrots at once on a strict schedule. There are eighteen thousand kids to feed. Plus, the district has only thirty cents per student to spend on vegetables per day. Zero percent of Madison school lunches are sourced locally."

"Wow." Zoe had done her research. I blinked at her, amazed.

"I've decided that I can't accomplish much alone, so I'm going to start volunteering with REAP Food Group when the harvesting is done here. They said that since

I'm so young, I could focus my efforts on, like, social networking to educate kids and teens. I might make another video, but this time for students instead of school boards."

"Cool. What does it stand for?"

"Um, Research, Education, Action, and Policy. They work with farmers on school lunch issues and sponsor chef visits to classrooms and stuff. It's awesome."

"Neat!" I was impressed. Zoe was already so accomplished on the tennis court and had always gotten straight A's. And now she was ready to make her mark on the food world. I gingerly pulled the little tomatoes off the vine and ate only every fifth one. Okay, every third one.

"Yeah. Except I told my parents all about it and they are not thrilled with the idea." Zoe sighed. She took off her gloves for a minute to wipe the tiniest bit of sweat off her face.

"What? Why not?"

"You know. They want me to, like, cure cancer or something. That doesn't leave a lot of extra time for local food activism." Zoe's parents were pretty intense about her grades and her tennis record. Over the summer they had seemed calmer, but now that the school year was about to begin, they must have been telling her there wasn't time for her new passion. She frowned. "They want me to start looking at colleges already."

"But that's the thing," I said. "Louisa's always saying that if people would just eat better, they wouldn't get sick as much. Maybe, in a sort of indirect way, you *will* cure cancer. With food."

Zoe smiled. "Maybe. But for some reason, no one gets very excited about *preventing* bad things from happening. Anyway, I need to finish up here and get out to the court. I have to play at least number two singles."

"As a freshman?" I knew that the best player on the team was usually in the number one singles slot. For Zoe to be number two as a new team member would be incredible.

"Yeah." Zo got that intense look on her face that appeared when she knew she had to do something tough.

"Zo? I know you can do anything you set your mind to. But . . . just . . . let's enjoy high school. You know what I mean?"

"Yeah. Hey, thanks for the help with the tomatoes."

"Anytime."

# SteepingLeafScone.com

### Plain Scones

This scone is inspired by my baking lesson with Tom Hines of Batch Bakehouse in downtown Madison. He taught me that the best treats are the ones with high-quality ingredients and lots of heart. Thank you, Mr. Hines, for reminding me that sometimes the best things in life are the simple things!

### Ingredients

2 cups King Arthur all-purpose flour
1 tablespoon baking powder
½ cup sugar
½ teaspoon salt
5 tablespoons Lurpack butter
1 fresh egg
⅔ cup fresh buttermilk
½ teaspoon secret ingredient
¼ cup whole milk

Preheat the oven to 400 degrees Fahrenheit. Mix the dry ingredients together first, then cut in the butter and egg. Slowly add the buttermilk to form a thick dough. Add the secret ingredient. Knead the dough on a board, roll to a 1-inch thickness, and cut the dough into 2-inch triangles. Place each triangle on a greased cookie sheet and brush the tops with milk. Bake for 12 to 15 minutes until golden brown; serve warm with clotted cream and jam or preserves. Makes 10 scones.

### Customer comments:

"Exquisite!" "Incredibly amazing." "Almost creamy . . ."

August 5  10:57 a.m.

## Chapter Twenty

My hour for tea is half-past five, and my buttered toast
waits for nobody.
—WILKIE COLLINS, *THE WOMAN IN WHITE*

I felt lucky that Zoe had forgiven me so quickly for being a less-than-great BFF. I figured it wouldn't hurt to go visit Genna, too. I biked from the community garden to the Matthews spread. I expected to find Gen out on the patio. But Sarah, the housekeeper, said she was in the basement.

"The basement?" I repeated. "But it's about eighty degrees and sunny. That only happens about two weeks out of the year here."

"I know. You should drag her outside," Sarah said with a slight eye roll. "I tried, but she wouldn't hear it."

"I'll do my best." I ran down the soft carpeted stairs.

The basement was gorgeous, all lush micro-suede furniture and impressive theateresque equipment for watching movies. But it was still a basement. What was Genna up to?

"There you are!" I found Gen in an area off the main room. The wall was mirrored and it was full of exercise equipment: her mom's fitness room. Genna was sweating on an elliptical.

"An . . . nie. Hey." She was out of breath. I thought she'd hop off, but she sped up instead.

"Gen, let's go to the zoo or something. It's gorgeous outside." I sat down on a huge rubber ball and started bouncing. I was pretty sure that wasn't what you were supposed to do with it.

"I . . . can't," she said, wheezing. "I'm . . . doing . . . one more . . . hour."

"Genna! That's a lot. How long have you been on that thing?"

She finally stopped. Thank God. "I dunno. A while. Look." She pointed. It was the latest glossy weekly magazine. Cecily Stevens was on the cover. In a bikini, looking way too skinny if you asked me.

"So? I thought James said she was a diva. And I thought you stopped reading those so much." I quit bouncing and looked at Genna more carefully. Her eyes seemed dull. "Genna, tell me you haven't stopped eating again.

I'm calling my mom." I scanned the room for Genna's phone . . . it couldn't be far away. Unfortunately, it sat on the elliptical's book holder.

"I'm eating! I'm just exercising a bit more too." Genna wouldn't meet my eyes; she knew she was busted.

"How much more?"

"Quite a bit. How come you never yell at Zoe for practicing so much?" she said defiantly.

"First of all, I'm not yelling. And I do worry about Zo sometimes. But she's really careful about eating enough food and drinking the right amount of water and stuff. I'm not sure if you are," I said gently. I knew Genna didn't need me getting all angry with her.

"I swear, I am eating. I had a smoothie an hour ago."

"Okay. I won't call my mom. But Genna, will you please stop worrying so much about being skinny? It's just . . . boring." It was.

She laughed. I exhaled in relief. "I know. It is. But I'm trying out for show choir and they wear these huge sequined blouses that are going to look ridiculous on me. I want to look good."

"You do look good. Please, please, please believe me," I pleaded with her. Genna was so pretty. Ever since we'd all been twelve, boys had followed her around. Why couldn't she see it?

"I believe you. It's just . . . I feel like you don't . . ."

"I don't what?"

"Like, live in the real world. Don't get mad. It's just that I really want to be an actress, and it's rough out there. Casting directors don't care how healthy you are. They just want a certain look. And *that* is it." She pointed at Cecily.

"Oh, Genna." I loved that Gen was so creative and talented. I thought that every single time I'd seen her onstage in anything, she'd been amazing. But why did she think that to go to the next level, she had to look like everyone else?

"It's just really hard. I'm already at a disadvantage because I don't live in New York or LA."

I wished that Genna could be happy with a healthy, slightly boring life here in Madison. But I was starting to accept that she never would. All I could do when she pushed herself to extremes was to try and push back a little. And listen.

I gave her a hug then, and talked her into coming out into the sun.

Dear readers,

Fruit teas are a great way to enjoy healthy foods in a fun way. Here's a fun fruit-infused iced tea recipe. It's super refreshing. Hope you like it! ☺

**Orange Strawberry Iced Tea**

**Ingredients**
⅔ cup brewed green tea (I used a ginger blend from Louisa, but any kind of green tea is fine)
⅔ cup orange juice
⅓ cup sliced strawberries
2 teaspoons sugar
⅓ cup ice cubes

In a large pint glass, place ice cubes. Add tea, juice, and sugar. Stir. Add sliced strawberries and enjoy!

<3 Annie

August 5  9:31 p.m.

## Chapter Twenty-One

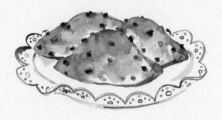

Tea. Earl Grey. Hot. And whoever this "Earl Grey" fellow is,
I'd like to have a word with him. . . .
—JEAN-LUC PICARD, STAR TREK: THE NEXT GENERATION

Two weeks flew by. I spent most of it baking, of course. I did decide to add a few bonus ingredients to my perfect scones, but I kept them a secret from everyone. I wasn't being suspicious; I just didn't want to jinx myself by being too sure that I'd go to the finals. Even though I chalked with Genna and Zoe again, handed out more fliers, and commented on practically every other blog on the entire Internet, SteepingLeafScone.com was stuck in seventh place on the leader board. SweetCakes kept inching up until it overtook first place from Master Baker. It seemed so unfair. The mean blog comments continued, but by now

I had so many nice followers leaving kind messages that SweetCakes didn't seem to matter as much. Especially when people started saying things like, "What is your problem?" to her.

Zach stayed away from the Leaf, but I did see him once, riding his bike down Monroe Street very slowly. Forgetting everything, I even waved to him. But I don't think he saw me. Or if he did, he didn't care. I wondered if we'd ever be friends again, if we had ever been friends in the first place.

There wasn't time to worry about it. I was so determined to get to Chicago that I'd started visiting neighbors and other Monroe Street businesses in person to tell them about my blog. I had to try absolutely everything. A nice woman from *Madison* magazine did a post about me on their website, and several restaurants around the square let me hang up little posters about the blog and the scone competition in their windows. I sure hoped it would pay off. I still hadn't purchased any new clothes for school *or* gotten a haircut. It seemed that my brain was on a constant loop repeating, *"Get-more-blog-followers-practice-baking-get-more-blog-followers-practice-baking . . ."*

Zoe still didn't make any headway with the Madison school board, but she burst into the Leaf one day when I was experimenting with a new scone glaze.

"Annie! The principal of a charter school in Mount Horeb called me. She saw my video on your blog!"

"OMG, that is awesome!" I was so excited for Zoe, of course, but also happy to hear I had blog readers in Mount Horeb, which was an adorable suburb about twenty minutes away. "What did she say?"

Zoe threw a pretend ball in the air and made a serving motion, grinning from ear to ear. "She said she was interested in sourcing some food locally. I put her in touch with Murphy Farms and Harmony Valley!"

"Wow. Those lucky kids are going to eat the best cottage cheese ever," I said. I rushed over to Zo to give her a hug. "Way to go!"

"She said she'd been researching the issue for a while and just got a federal grant. So now it's just a matter of logistics . . . getting food directly from the farm to the school every week. Fortunately, the school has its own kitchen, which is incredible. It'll make it a lot easier."

"That sounds amazing." It was a great victory for local food and for Zoe! I was so proud of my friend. I wished we lived in a warmer climate so she could garden all year long.

Genna and James broke up. I couldn't believe it when Gen breezed into the Leaf to announce it, perfectly calm. I expected her to be devastated, but she said that she was getting bored of having a relationship of just texts. The real story was that when she tried out for show choir at West High, a cute sophomore named Sam had caught her eye, with his "adorable jazz hands." They'd already started rehearsing even though the first day of school was more than two weeks away. I was just happy that Genna seemed to have forgotten about Cecily Stevens and her too-skinny arms. For the moment.

The day before the eight a.m. deadline, SteepingLeaf Scone.com was not in the top five. I couldn't believe it. We were only nineteen blog followers behind Miss CuppyCake, who was in fifth place with 557 followers. In a last-ditch attempt to qualify for the Chicago bake-off, I asked every one of my best regular Steeping Leaf customers and supporters to come to the teashop. Ling brought Hieu and her husband. Oliver and Theresa came in. The Kopinskis arrived, and Mr. Silverman was there via Skype from Europe on Beth's laptop. Mr. Arun was there, as was the owner of Samadhi Spa. My mom, dad, sister, and brothers all arrived. Genna and Zoe came, of course, and Louisa gave us all a pep talk.

"As you all know, our dear Annie has worked very, very hard on her wonderful food blog. I couldn't be more proud of her efforts. Not only has she reached out to the community once again, but she's invented some truly

original and delicious recipes. We're so close to qualify-
ing for the final bake-off!" Everyone clapped and smiled
at me.

I continued. "I need all of you to do your best to help
me this evening." I went to the laptop and pulled up the
leader board. "As you can see, we are not in the top five.
I need some new blog followers before tomorrow, and
chances are, I'll need more than nineteen. The numbers
are constantly changing. We keep trading slots, and the
top five seem to be working hard tonight also to maintain
their lead. Please spend a little time calling or e-mailing
your friends and family and ask them to support us! If
you can think of anyone with a blog of their own, please
have them do a quick post about our contest."

Everyone clapped again. There was a lot of rustling
as people pulled out their phones and began dialing and
texting. Since I had already called, e-mailed, or visited
everyone I had ever met (and lots of people I hadn't), I
decided to make sure everyone was well hydrated while
they helped out. I went behind the counter and got busy
making pots of tea and delivering them around the shop.

Genna looked up from her phone after a few minutes
and said she couldn't think of anyone else to call. "But I
know you have a lot of followers in New York already,"
she assured me, looking sad. "I sent out an e-mail to the

whole theater camp list last week. And I texted everyone in my phone, my dad's phone, my mom's phone, and our housekeeper's phone. Sam said he did the same."

"That's okay, Gen. The important thing is that we've done everything we could think of. And it's so great that all these people are here trying to help."

Zoe had borrowed her brother's phone for the night and texted everyone in his address book. "Too bad we're not in school, actually. We could put posters on everyone's locker like the cheerleaders do before a big tournament."

"I like that idea. Oh well," I said wistfully. I refilled pots and thanked everyone for coming. Eventually it was time for people to go. I planned to help Louisa lock up, and walk back home with my family.

SteepingLeafScone.com did get five or six new followers over the course of the evening, but because everyone who had gathered had already helped spread the word earlier, it was hard to find new people who hadn't heard about the blog. The leaders kept pulling further ahead, and I started to accept that maybe we were at the end of the road. I guess I'd finally have time to get a haircut. Maybe I'd help Zoe with her harvest too.

I'm ashamed to admit I felt a tiny bit relieved when I went to bed and saw that SteepingLeafScone.com was in seventh place. All along I'd been nervous about going to Chicago and not only having to bake in front of other people and cameras in a strange place (on*stage*), but also talk to the judges.

And meet SweetCakes.

I'd been so worried that the moment I laid eyes on her, I'd lose my cool and, like, cry or something. But now it seemed I wouldn't have to do any of that. I felt the adrenaline drain out of my body. The relief mixed with disappointment as I thought about how hard I had worked to learn to become a credible baker and blogger. How could it all be for nothing?

# SteepingLeafScone.com

Dear readers,

The end of the contest is coming up soon. We're almost there! Just a few more followers here means I'll get to go to Chicago in September. Please tell your friends and family to visit the blog and consider following me if they like what they read. I'd love to have a chance to go to the finals and show the world what the Steeping Leaf and the Teashop Girls are all about!

Thank you so much for the support you've given me over the last several weeks. Hugs to you all. ☺ ☺ ☺

<3 Annie

August 20  10:14 p.m.

## Chapter Twenty-Two

More and more clearly as the scones disappeared into his interior
he saw that what the sensible man wanted was a wife and a home
with scones like these always at his disposal.
—P. G. WODEHOUSE, *BACHELORS ANONYMOUS*

The morning of the contest deadline, I did something different from what I'd done all the previous mornings for the last month. I didn't go to the computer within five minutes of waking up to check the leader board. Instead I calmly brushed my teeth, made a mug of tea, and stepped out onto the front porch. I didn't think about anything specific. I just watched a squirrel run around our driveway. I walked over to our lilac bush and took a deep breath. It felt kind of good to just notice the day beginning. Since it was only 6:30 a.m., my entire family was still asleep. I knew the house would start creaking and groaning with their movements very soon, but in the meantime, it was nice to have the morning all to myself. It was dewy and fresh.

I couldn't believe I'd be starting high school in a little over two weeks. There was so much to do. I'd already gotten my schedule but hardly even looked at it. I should have been thinking about what clubs I wanted to join or if I wanted to audition for the concert choir. I still needed to get some new clothes and some school supplies. Soon I'd be doing homework and only working at the Leaf on the weekends and one night per week. Thank goodness Theresa had mentioned the night before she'd be interested in picking up some shifts. She'd be so easy to train, thanks to her love of tea and her pleasant demeanor.

I sat on our rocking chair and kind of zoned out . . . maybe I'd gotten up a little *too* early. Suddenly the silence of the morning was pierced by a shout from down the block.

*"ANNIE!"*

I sat up straight, then bolted out of the chair when I heard Zoe's voice again. I stepped off the porch to see her running at full speed toward me. She was wearing white pajama pants and a white tank top, which made me worried something was wrong. I ran toward her to find out what was going on. I knew Zo got up early, but she usually managed to get dressed before she left her house.

"Aughhhhh! Annie, OMG, thank God you are awake.

We have to get to a computer! SteepingLeafScone.com got a bunch of new followers during the night. You're almost in the top five. We have to do something!" She grabbed my hand and pulled me back toward my house. We barreled toward the desktop in the living room. She bounced from foot to foot as I turned it on.

"I can't believe it!" I cried. I jumped up and down too, waiting to see for myself what Zoe was so excited about.

Finally, finally, the computer warmed up and I clicked on the browser. The leader page appeared and showed that SteepingLeafScone.com had gotten forty-seven new blog followers during the night! With sixty-eight minutes left to go before the deadline, we were only TWO FOLLOWERS AWAY from the last finalist slot.

"Aughhhh!" I yelled, not caring who I woke up. "It's true! What do I do?"

"There have to be two people out there somewhere who will bump you into the finalist round. Call Genna."

I was already on the phone. Genna was way groggy when she answered her phone on my second try, but when she understood what was happening, she quickly promised she would be right over. Five minutes later, she ran into my living room, also wearing pajama pants. Her hair was in a ponytail on top of her head. My parents came down the stairs and looked at us all quizzically.

"SteepingLeafScone.com is back in the running! We're only two followers behind!" Mom poured some coffee and Dad rubbed his eyes. My parents were not morning people.

"Okay, I have an idea," Genna said. "We have a little less than an hour. We've already called everyone we know, so we have to get some people we don't know. I'm going to start calling in to radio shows. I'll try 105.5 first." She sat down at the computer and began going to local shows' websites to find the right phone numbers.

"Great idea!" Zoe said. "Annie, do you have a radio?"

The only radio I ever listened to at all was in my parents' car, and it was always tuned to NPR. "Mom, do we have a radio in the house?"

"Um, yes. Hold on." She got up and began pushing buttons on the stereo, which had a radio but got really bad reception.

"Let me see if I can find my old boom box," my dad offered.

"Quick!" I said, then, "Sorry. Please." I was still bouncing around, and the tea I'd had wasn't even caffeinated. Finally, my dad pulled a dusty boom box out of the closet and extended the antenna. We all walked outside so it would work better. He tuned it to 105.5, Triple M.

Genna had already punched the number into her phone and was on hold.

We all stared at her. Would this work, or should I be trying something else? Genna started talking. Zoe turned the volume on the radio down. She must've gotten through to a producer. She explained the situation and got put on hold again.

"Hi, Triple M?" I suppressed a yelp. It sounded like Genna had gotten through to the show host. "Do you like scones?"

Genna, using her best mature actress voice, explained to the 105.5 DJ that we needed the listeners' help. The morning show host was a complete darling and repeated the blog address on air. Within minutes I saw our follower numbers climb. By the time eight a.m. arrived, SteepingLeafScone.com was in fourth place on the leader board.

Louisa and I were going to Chicago.

YAY, YAY, YAY!

Dear readers,

Well, I didn't think it was going to happen, but WE'RE GOING TO CHICAGO!!!! I'm SO EXCITED. I couldn't have done it without you. Thank you so much for your support. I'll be leaving soon for the finals with my family. Genna and Zoe are coming too; we're all thrilled. I've asked Genna to live-blog the event so you can be with us the whole way. The next two weeks are going to be busy, busy, busy perfecting *the* perfect recipe for the competition.

YAYAYAYAY!

Love, Annie

August 21  8:05 a.m.

## Chapter Twenty-Three

He refused tea, but Mrs. Crowley poured out a cup and handed it to him. "You need not drink it, but I insist on your holding it in your hand. I hate people who habitually deny themselves things."
—W. Somerset Maugham, *The Explorer*

No one wanted to miss the excitement of a trip to Chicago, so Gen, Zoe, and Beth piled into the minivan. I squeezed into the far back with my friends, Beth and Louisa shared the middle seat, and my parents were up front. Billy and Luke were extremely upset that they wouldn't get to go, but my mom said we'd do a special trip to a water park in Wisconsin Dells next weekend, and that made them happy. They were going to spend the day with one of our incredibly patient neighbors.

The van was packed. We didn't road-trip very often, so we erred on the side of bringing too much stuff. My mom had a little cooler filled with iced tea and string cheese, and Beth carried an enormous purse filled with a knitting project, iPod, and at least eleven magazines. I was pleased they were all *Vanity Fair*s and *New Yorker*s and didn't have pictures of too-skinny teenagers on the front.

"Do you have the GPS, hon?" my mom asked my dad. He was navigating.

"Yep, right here. Er, just a sec." He double-checked and ran back into the house.

"What about the pass for the tolls?" We were borrowing a speed pass from one of his coworkers.

"Got it!" My dad checked the visor to make sure the pass was where he thought it was. "Wait a minute." He ran back into the house. I really hoped we made it in time. Good thing my grandmother would be around to remind me to breathe.

Louisa brought only a small satchel, but Genna made up for any extra space in the van by bringing practically the entire contents of her bedroom with us. I wasn't sure if I was entering a baking contest or a beauty pageant, but I sure was glad to have her along.

The first thing you need to know about the day of the competition was that my hair looked like something out of a horror film. I knew that when I baked my scone later, someone would probably be taping me. I wanted to look nice, of course, and my hair was so long that it had taken over my body. So I borrowed Beth's flat iron.

Bad idea.

The little iron was no match for my head of thick, curly hair. It burned out when I was only about half-done, so I had one side of completely (okay, not *completely*) straight hair and one side of curly hair. *Why? Why? Why?*

"But my hair is a total disaster!" I yelled at my dad when it was really and truly time to go. I was staring at myself in the mirror by the front door, trying a last-ditch attempt to fix it by adding leave-in conditioner.

"Your hair is perfect, kiddo. We have to roll," he said. When it comes to hair, dads may as well be blind.

"Annie, I'll fix it when we get there. I promise," Genna said, pulling me to the van.

"It's not *that* bad," Zoe added. I shot her a look, and she quickly said, "Okay, it is."

"Can't we fix it in the car? We could plug your flat iron into the lighter," I suggested hopefully.

"I don't have an adapter. Plus, the cord won't reach that far. Don't worry, we'll have plenty of time, and I'm a genius with hair. Besides, if we can't get all your hair straight, we'll just stick your head under a faucet and make the whole thing curly again." I sighed at the unfairness of life but got into the van. Genna had a huge tote with hair products. In fact, it was so huge that it took up more space in the back of the van than my cooler of scone ingredients. My dad was not pleased when he saw the packing challenge, but we made it work.

All the way down, my family was in high spirits.

"You know what the difference is between a scone and a biscuit?" my dad called back to me.

"I have no idea, Dad," I said, with a teeny eye roll at Gen and Zo.

"Two bucks!" he said, cracking up.

"Very funny."

"Did we remember the camera?" my mom asked. She was still in packing mode . . . and I think she was nervous for me.

"I've got it, Mom," Beth said.

"Thank you."

"Louisa, have you had tea in Chicago?" Genna asked. "I went to the Drake Hotel for tea once when I was little. I can't remember why, but it was really nice."

"Oh, the Palm Court. Yes, I've been many times. Annie's grandfather and I used to love going to Chicago on the weekends. Hear the symphony, stroll through the Art Institute. I should see if Davis would like to go this fall . . ." She trailed off, smiling.

"I'm sure he would," I said. "And if Mr. Arun won't, *I'd* go anytime."

"Wonderful, Annie," Louisa said.

"As soon as I get my driver's license," I added. I heard my mom groan.

My dad started pointing out license plates from states other than Wisconsin the minute we got on the interstate. Even though it was a game for kids, we all got into it when we saw a plate from Rhode Island. "Wow," Zoe said. "They've been in the car a long time."

While my family laughed and joked, I got more and more nervous. Zoe must have seen the look on my face, because she put her arm around me and said, "Annie. It's going to be fine. When you're making your scone, don't think of anyone else in the room. Just focus on what you're doing. Pretend you're inside the Steeping Leaf. When I have to play tennis in a big tournament with lots of spectators, I totally block them out."

Genna piped up, "Me too. When I'm onstage, I never look at the audience at all. It's just me and the other people in the scene. It'll just be you and the flour, Annie."

I smiled weakly and my stomach churned. I wasn't sure if it would have been better to have skipped breakfast or eaten more of it. Yuck.

"We're all very proud of you, dear," Louisa said. Even

Beth nodded in agreement. She was listening to her iPod, but I guess it was on at low volume.

I did some deep calming breaths and felt a little better. Until, that is, Genna's phone made its signature beeping sound. "Weird. It's a text for *you*, Annie."

She handed over the phone and I read it. "Break a mixer. —Z."

I showed it to Zoe. "Is he trying to be nice?"

"I doubt it," she said.

"Aw, sure he is," Genna said. "I mean, just the fact that he knew today is the day of the bake-off is sweet. He's not so bad, Annie."

"Genna, he was totally spying on me for SweetCakes!" I cried.

"Hmm," was all she had to say to that.

Finally, the beautiful Chicago skyline loomed ahead of us as we cruised toward the big city on I-90. The bake-off was to be held in the ballroom of a hotel in one of the northwest suburbs. My mom drove and my dad navigated, and we managed to arrive without mishap. Louisa promised she'd get us set up in the ballroom with my parents and Beth so I'd have a few minutes to deal with my hair before meeting the other contestants. She was so amazing. We hopped out of the van and I hugged her before racing off with Gen and Zo to the nearest bathroom. There was no way I could face SweetCakes looking like a total freak.

Genna plugged in the flat iron and we all stared at it, willing it to get hotter faster. While that was happening, Gen dug in her bag for some powder. She started brushing it on my face, but my cheeks and freckles blazed right through it. I always turned red when I was nervous.

"How about some eyeliner?" she suggested.

"I don't know, Genna. I'm not used to wearing anything on my eyes. What if I rub it during the thing and smear a black stripe across my head?"

Zoe laughed. "Just give her some lip gloss and that's it, Genna."

Genna sighed, resigned. She was reaching for the flat iron when the bathroom door banged open. A girl who looked quite a bit younger than us walked in, barely even glancing in our direction, but then something made her stop. She turned toward me, and I saw her nametag.

The first line said *Lily*.

The second line said *SweetCakes*.

# SteepingLeafScone.com

Dear readers,

As you can imagine, I'm pretty nervous. If you have any advice about calming jitters, please share. I'm drinking a lot of chamomile tea, and it is helping a little bit. In the meantime, I wanted to share with you one more page from my Teashop Girls Handbook.

This ad reminds me of the stories Louisa told me about her grandmother Sarah (my great-great-grandmother!). Sarah started a weekly tea with her best friends and fellow suffragists, and they continued the tradition for many, many years after women won the right to vote in 1920.

I like this ad because it shows how nothing really changes. I mean, I know that Genna and Zoe and I don't usually wear gowns and use fine silver for our weekly teas, but it's still the same idea. Just a bunch of awesome (if I do say so myself) girls getting together to eat and drink yummy things. And Jell-O is definitely a yummy thing . . . hmmm, Idea of the Week: Try making Jell-O with green tea!

<3 Annie

September 4  6:08 a.m.

## Chapter Twenty-Four

Oh my dear fellow . . . should you not be asking,
"Would the tea like the cup?"
—Oscar Wilde

The first thing that popped into my mind was that I was glad I had Gen and Zo with me to face her. The second thing was the state of my hair. The third was the fact that the nemesis who'd had me in such a tizzy for over a month was just a kid.

"How old are you?" I blurted, without even thinking.

"What?" She narrowed her eyes. SweetCakes had thin brown hair parted in the middle of her head. She wore glasses with black rims and a plain blue dress. "I'm ten. What's it to you?"

"I'm Annie. From SteepingLeafScone.com." I couldn't

help it—I smiled. It was impossible to be intimidated now that I knew SweetCakes was so young. I felt foolish for being so bugged by her.

"You're going down," she said, and spun on her heel to leave. "Nice hair."

"Sweet kid," Genna said after she'd gone.

"Jeez," Zoe added.

"I can't believe I was so worried about that," I finished. Genna and Zoe exchanged a look. I realized that both of them were a lot more experienced than me when it came to competition. Zoe had faced countless tennis foes, and Genna had tried out for tons of plays. They seemed to be saying, *Don't count your chickens before they're hatched.* "I mean, I'm sure she's a fine baker. But she's not nearly as scary as I expected her to be in person."

"You'll do great, Annie. Now, let's finish your hair." Genna pulled me closer to the sinks and got to work.

My hair was not straight when Gen was through with it. It was just a more subdued version of its normal self. I'd made her stop when the strands started steaming. I didn't want to head into the ballroom with a black flat-iron-shaped singe on the side of my head.

## Things to Not Forget During the Bake-Off

- Smile
- Go slow, there's plenty of time
- Don't worry about the crowd or the other bakers
- Smile
- Try to have fun
- Don't forget the baking soda

The ballroom was gorgeous. Huge crystal chandeliers hung every twenty feet, and five elaborate baking stations were set up on a slightly elevated platform. Each one had its own oven, stove, counter, sink, and rolling baker's racks. My family had registered me and unloaded all of my ingredients, so all I had to do was pin on my name tag and check in with the judges. The baking would start in a half hour.

Before we began, there was something I wanted to do. I introduced myself to the three competitors I hadn't met yet. Each one of them was incredibly nice and complimentary. They'd all visited my blog multiple times and told me how good it was. Two of them were older girls, both sixteen, and one—Scone-y Nation—was a boy about my age. You could tell he took himself very seriously, because he wore a huge chef's hat and seemed to have no idea that it looked a bit strange on him. Finally, I went over to SweetCakes's station. She was on one end, and no one else would talk to her. It seemed I wasn't the only victim of her mean comments.

"Hi again," I said to her. "It's Lily?"

She glared at me. How could such a young person be so unpleasant? I decided to ignore her glare and pushed on.

"We met before in the bathroom?" I prodded, as if she might have forgotten something that happened ten minutes ago.

"Your hair looks worse," she said. I frowned. This was clearly pointless.

"Listen, I was just going to wish you luck, but never mind. Your mean comments online and rudeness now aren't going to help you with the judges. And spying on me isn't going to help either. There's no reason you have to be like this. It was supposed to be fun." My words came out in an indignant rush.

She didn't say a word for a long time. Eventually, I began to walk away. When I had taken about five steps, I heard her say, "I wasn't spying."

I turned back toward her. "You weren't? How did you know my secret ingredient, then?"

"You're obsessed with tea. Duh. What *else* would it be?"

I felt my face redden.

It didn't matter anymore, so I gave up and went back to my own baking station. The important thing now was to put it out of my head and get down to business. My family sat down in some nice cushiony chairs in the second row. Genna and Zoe sat next to them. The ballroom was full of people. Camerapeople took their spots and a few local newspaper reporters began interviewing the judges. I smoothed my hair and checked my dress, which was pale pink and lovely. It was Beth's dress from her sophomore year spring-fling dance, and I was touched when she gave it to me to wear. I'd always loved it. I tied my yellow Steeping Leaf apron on and took some more deep breaths. Soon it would be time to bake.

Dear readers,

This is Genna Matthews blogging to you directly from Chicago. The hotel where the competition is being held is very nice, although we just ran into one of Annie's competitors in the bathroom and it wasn't all hugs and kisses, if you catch my drift. But that's okay, we've got Annie ready and looking GORGEOUS if I do say so myself, so I know this thing is IN THE BAG. I better start practicing my British accent so we fit right in in London. Anyway, Annie is about to take the stage. More soon!

XOXOX, Genna

September 4  12:30 p.m.

## Chapter Twenty-Five

I can give you a cup of tea in no time—
and you won't meet any bores.
—EDITH WHARTON, *THE HOUSE OF MIRTH*

A master of ceremonies took the stage and welcomed everyone to the first annual Duchess Tea Company Scone Bake-Off. He wore a tuxedo even though it was only two p.m. His hair was black and slicked back. First, he introduced all of the contestants. I noticed that all of us had major cheering sections . . . all of us except for Lily. I decided to put her out of my mind. And not just Lily. I stopped looking at the crowd in front of the stage and at the emcee. I shut my eyes for a brief moment and thought about the scone I was about to make.

I'd settled on a terrific recipe with small bits of toffee

and green apple. I also planned to make a delicate glaze for the top. And I had more than just Tom's bakery wisdom up my sleeve. When Louisa heard the incredible news a couple of days ago that we were going to Chicago, she said she had something special for me.

"I know you've been making your scones with as few delectable ingredients as possible, dear," she explained. "But if you do decide to add a pinch of tea for good luck, I have just the one."

I opened the beautiful box she presented and saw that it contained a small portion of oolong tea leaves.

"It's Tieguanyin, dearest," Louisa said with a smile. I gasped.

"I couldn't possibly . . . I . . . wow." Tieguanyin is a Chinese tea named for a Buddhist god. It's the most valuable tea in the world, because it is grown on just one mountain and harvested on only one day per year. I didn't even know that Louisa had it.

"I insist you enjoy it, love. You can put it in your recipe or drink it along with your finished scone."

I whispered, "Thank you," and a wonderful feeling of certainty had settled over me. I was *ready*.

But now, in the middle of things, I felt less certain. With a grand gesture the master of ceremonies told us to begin baking, and we all got to work. It was really hard for me not to lose precious minutes by glancing at my competitors, but I forced myself to concentrate on my own scones. I mixed my dry ingredients first and then slowly added the wet ones. I cut my pristine green apple into very small pieces and added them to the mix. Next, the toffee pieces went in. I was careful not to add too many, because I wanted them to complement, not over-whelm, the scone. Finally, I added a pinch of Tieguanyin that I'd ground ahead of time using Louisa's mortar and pestle. I didn't know if the judges would be able to taste it, but just knowing that it was there made me happy. I smiled as I mixed everything up.

When the dough was ready, I patted it into an inch-thick slab and began cutting it into small triangles. I placed them all on a baking sheet, and into the oven it went. I turned my attention to the brown butter tea glaze. First, I brewed two tablespoons of the Tieguanyin tea. I put it in a metal bowl over ice. When it cooled, I melted and slightly browned Lurpak butter and added it to the bowl. Next came a cup and a half of confectioners' sugar, one half teaspoon of vanilla, and two tablespoons of whole milk. I stirred it all together. It smelled heavenly.

Actually, the entire ballroom was beginning to smell heavenly. Now that my glaze was finished and the scones were in the oven and close to being done, I could relax a little bit. I looked at my family and at the Teashop Girls. They all waved and flashed thumbs-ups. I waved back, even though I knew it made me look like a dork. The baker next to me, one of the older girls, was making a savory scone. I could smell garlic and cheese. On the other side I saw leftover berries. I knew that the judges were in for some real treats. I couldn't see what Lily was making, but I was sure it was good.

I thought about what she had said about not spying on me. Was it true? Had I simply imagined it? I felt embarrassed. I didn't want to apologize to Zach for accusing him of selling me out, but it looked like I was probably going to have to. I hated feeling ridiculous. But it was his fault too! It's not like it was *normal* for him to go and kiss me out of the blue. You couldn't blame a girl for freaking out a little. I sighed. Why did boys have to be so difficult?

Two minutes later, the judges called time. My scones were a perfect golden brown. I'd checked the time limit ahead, so I'd cut them the right size to cook in time. It was part of all my practicing. One other baker, the boy in the chef's hat, immediately started protesting. He'd made his lemon scones too big and they weren't quite done yet. I felt bad for him. It would be very tough for him to win if his insides were gooey. But the judges were firm. We had to plate our scones.

I presented mine on a cute blue polka-dotted plate. I carefully poured the glaze in a zigzag pattern. We could get additional points for presentation, so I knew it was important to use a steady hand. My glaze turned out perfect, and I wanted to squeal. Things were going so well!

All five of us presented our scones to the three judges and held our breath.

# SteepingLeafScone.com

Dear readers,

It smells amazing in this ballroom. The scones are coming out of the ovens and Annie's looks incredible. It's made with perfect fall ingredients and has this to-die-for glaze. The judges are trying everything now, OMG, it is so exciting.

Okay, now they're taking FOREVER to talk amongst themselves. How hard can it be, people? It's so obvious Annie is the winner, right?

Right?

Right?

Blog readers, if you're out there, please send every positive vibe you've got!!! The entire audience is on the edge of our seats. And we're all pretty hungry.

XOXOX, Genna

September 4  2:41 p.m.

## Chapter Twenty-Six

Have you got everything you need in the shape of—of tea?
—F. Scott Fitzgerald, *The Great Gatsby*

The three judges tried all five scones and took copious notes. Seriously, what were they writing down? We were allowed to sit with our friends and family again, so I waited with Genna, Zoe, Louisa, Beth, and my parents. I could not stop tapping my foot. Finally, Beth reached over and held my leg down. She also said it would be great if I could stop sweating in her dress. I said, "No promises."

Everyone congratulated me on finishing my recipe perfectly and I beamed. I wanted to win very badly, but even if I didn't, I felt great about how the day had gone so far. I had done what I came here to do, and SweetCakes hadn't even made me cry.

The judges all huddled together for what felt like an eternity. Finally, the little cluster broke up and they filed onto the stage. First, one of them said a few words thanking us all for participating and how impressed they were with our baking skills and how much Duchess Tea loved collaborating with bakers and young people blah, blah, blah. All five of us were practically bouncing out of our chairs. We wanted to know who WON!

Then, they spent another nine years thanking all of the sponsors and giving a long-winded history of high tea and the invention of the scone. Normally, of course, I would have enjoyed such a thing, but under the circumstances I could have done without it. Since Beth wouldn't let me tap my foot, I started tapping my fingers on the chair. She crossed her eyes at me. I crossed mine back. We giggled. Then, Zoe and Genna started giggling too. We were all pretty tense.

The head judge then cleared his throat into the microphone, and we all sat up straight. Someone pressed a button on a keyboard and the ballroom filled with the sound of a synthesized drumroll.

"In third place . . . Master Baker with her cheesy garlic scone!" People clapped. I saw her rise to collect her ribbon and year's supply of scone ingredients. She looked sad but smiled bravely. My heart sped up a notch.

"In second place . . . SteepingLeafScone with her apple toffee scone!" I gasped. What? No! This couldn't be right. I couldn't be second! Second place didn't get to go to London with her two best friends. Second place . . . I realized that everyone's eyes were on me. I couldn't cry. I heard Louisa say, "Congratulations, my dearest dear." She gave me a squeeze. My dad clapped and whooped. "Yay, Annie!" I had to go to the stage. Genna and Zoe gave me hugs that were both congratulatory and comforting. "Great job, Annie," Zoe said. They knew I was disappointed, but they were proud of me for placing. I stood and collected my ribbon. I also won a beautiful pink Kitchen Aid mixer. My dad came up to help me carry it off the stage. I smiled, genuinely, and sat back down. I couldn't believe it was over. Louisa gave me a big hug, and my mom leaned over to say, "I'm so very proud of you, honey."

The fake drumroll sounded again.

"In first place . . . the winner of the all-expenses-paid trip to London . . . SweetCakes with her delicious cherry scone!"

Dear readers,

AUGHGHGHGHGHGH! Annie came in second. NOOOOOOOOO!

This can't be happening.

The girl who was mean in the bathroom, SweetCakes, won first place. I DEMAND A RECOUNT.

XOXOX, Genna

September 4    3:04 p.m.

## Chapter Twenty-Seven

Sadly, I swallowed my tea and stared at the crowd of
second-rate elegance . . .
—HERMANN HESSE, *STEPPENWOLF*

The crowd clapped, but there was a deep silence
from all of the competitors. I caught Master
Baker's eye, and she frowned. I knew what she
was thinking. It was the same thing all of us were thinking: *no fair.* SweetCakes had been a terrible competitor:
intimidating and mean. It was awful to see a person like
that come out ahead, even if she was only ten. Now she'd
feel that acting that way was perfectly justified. I shook
my head, disbelieving. I watched as Lily walked up to the
stage, looking smug. She accepted a huge trophy from
Duchess Tea with a teacup on top (I *wanted* that thing)
and took a deep bow. Her parents whistled and snapped a

million pictures. When she finally stopped bowing, I saw some reporters go up to her. I just kept staring.

Well, kiddo. That's all she wrote. Should we get packed up?" My dad squeezed my shoulders consolingly. He wore a T-shirt that said "TEAM STEEPING LEAF." My mom had one too; my dad had had them made up special yesterday.

"I guess so." I didn't feel like gathering my things and going back to Madison. I knew that Genna and Zoe had planned a special party for me at the Leaf. I also knew that it was *supposed* to be a victory party. It was going to be hard to be cheery with my second-place ribbon. Especially when so many folks in Madison had supported me and my blog.

I stood up and took off my yellow apron. It had been a good day, even without a triumphant victory.

Something caught my eye as I went to the stage to get my bowls. Miss Cuppycake and Scone-y Nation were talking animatedly to the judges. They had a laptop computer and were pointing at it. I walked closer to hear what they were saying.

"You have to take a few minutes and check these!" Scone-y Nation (a.k.a. Tim) was saying. "Some of these blog followers are not real people. Look!"

One of the judges was mostly ignoring him, but

another was paying attention. Miss Cuppycake (Shana) chimed in next. "All you have to do is look at the e-mail addresses matched to the blog followers. A lot of them are way too similar. We think SweetCakes cheated."

I gasped. Was it possible? The judges spent a few minutes looking at the computer. They signaled to the emcee. After a hushed conversation the emcee climbed the stage and asked for everyone's attention.

"Er, excuse me. It seems there have been some . . . irregularities on the blogs, ladies and gentlemen. The judges have asked that everyone remain in the ballroom for thirty minutes while they double-check the legitimacy of the competitors' blog followers."

There was intense murmuring throughout the entire room. My eyes were saucers when I returned from the stage with my bowls and ingredients. Genna and Zoe were jumping up and down.

"Annie! I bet her followers were totally all fake! What if it means you won?" Genna squealed.

"I can't believe they didn't check this before," Zoe said, all business. "What kind of show are these people running?"

We all settled back into our chairs to wait. I sure was glad that each and every one of my blog followers was a real person. It never even occurred to me to register new e-mail addresses and follow myself. What an under-handed trick! I scanned the room for SweetCakes, and there she was in the front row, looking defiant. Her parents were both on cell phones. Probably calling their lawyers, I thought. This was crazy.

The judges emerged from whatever secret room they'd hidden in and took the stage again.

"Ladies and gentlemen, we apologize for this unexpected delay," the emcee said. "After consulting with our webmaster and several other experts, we are sorry to announce that our winner has been disqualified for cheating.

"I'd like to announce a new first-place winner. Annie Green, of SteepingLeafScone, you are going to London!"

Dear readers,

MAJOR, MAJOR developments, people. SweetCakes has been dethroned. She cheated. I know, I'm stunned too. (Not really.)

More to come!

AHHHHHHHHHHHHHHHHHHHH!

THEY JUST ANNOUNCED ANNIE WON! ANNIE WON! WE'RE GOING TO LONDON!!!!!!!!!!!!!!!!!!!!!!!!!!!!!!!!!!!!!!!!!!!!!!!!!!!!!!!!!!!!!!

XOXOX, Genna

September 4   3:55 p.m.

## Chapter Twenty-Eight

Tea, for me, is one of the great subjects. It is a romantic trade, it does not pollute excessively, it has all sorts of health benefits, it calms and wakes you up at the same time.
—ALEXANDER McCALL SMITH

AUGHHHHHHHHHHHHHHH!" Genna, Zoe, and I screamed our heads off. We finally had to take a breath and then we started shrieking again. Finally, Beth rolled her eyes and pushed me to the stage. I ran up there. The judges high-fived me. The crowd applauded. From the front row, Lily and her parents glared at me. But I didn't care.

WE WON!

The rest of the day went by in a total blur. I collected my prize and teacup trophy and got interviewed by the reporters (I hoped I managed to sound coherent). I ran back to my family and hugged everyone about four times. Louisa was particularly excited for me. As soon as all of our shouting quieted, I remembered to thank her again for the special tea.

"I think it was the Tieguanyin, Louisa. That's why we won."

"I think it was more than that, dearest. You put all of your heart into your scones." Louisa gave me a squeeze. "In the end, *that* was the secret ingredient."

"I did. But I couldn't have done it without you and the Teashop Girls."

"Most things worth doing require a little help. I'm so proud of you, my sweet."

After that, all there was left to do was drive home to Madison. I was so glad now that Genna and Zoe had planned a party. I wanted to celebrate all night long. The entire ride home, Genna texted people to let them know what had happened. She promised me that the Leaf would be full when we returned to it.

"There's one thing I don't get, though," Zoe said thoughtfully. "How did SteepingLeafScone.com get all of those extra blog followers the night before the deadline?"

"Yeah," Genna said. "How *did* that happen? Beth, did you do something?"

Beth turned around in her seat. "I got everyone I know to follow it way before the deadline."

"Louisa?"

"It's a mystery, dears. Most of my friends think the Internet is a government conspiracy and won't touch the thing." She winked to let us know she was kidding. But I knew that Louisa wouldn't have waited until the last minute if she'd had some special plan up her sleeve. And she wouldn't have kept it a secret from me.

We all sat in silence for a minute, mentally going over the possibilities. Finally, Genna squirmed and I saw that she had a sly grin on her face. She immediately began working her phone, her thumbs flying over the tiny keyboard.

"What's with you?" Zoe said.

"Nothing," was all Genna would reply.

Zoe and I kept trying to grab her phone to see who she had texted, but she managed to keep it away from us. I resigned myself to finding out what she was up to when she was good and ready for me to find out.

When our van pulled up to the Leaf, I saw that it was no ordinary evening at the teashop. My eyes teared a little when I saw that someone had already hung up a banner that said CONGRATULATIONS, ANNIE!

"Louisa, who ran the store while we were gone all day?" I asked.

"Davis and Theresa. Looks like they did a splendid

job," she replied. Sure enough, there was my school principal pouring tea. I could see all of our neighbors, friends, and regular customers in the shop and spilling out of it. Someone was playing reggae music, which was perfect. It was a hot September night.

I hopped out of the van, and immediately people came up to offer their well-wishes. I reached for our cooler and began handing out the winning scones. Luke and Billy jumped on me when they saw the food. I gave them each two. And another one to Mr. Arun. My dad and mom carried all of my bowls and equipment back into the shop. There would be a lot of dishes to do. But not tonight.

Tonight was all about celebration. I tied my yellow apron back on over my pink dress and made sure my parents and Gen and Zo had delicious iced chais to drink. Next, I put out our party lanterns and lit some candles. Everyone kept coming up to congratulate me. I collected hugs from what felt like the entire Dudgeon-Monroe neighborhood and half of the university. It was wonderful. And this wasn't even the best part. The best part was the prize itself: London! I couldn't even think about it without feeling like floating off the ground. It was going to be tea *paradise*.

Just then, I spotted someone I didn't expect to see.

Zach Anderson pushed through the crowd. I almost

made a quick escape to the bathroom, but it was too late. I could see that he'd spotted me.

"Green. I hear your terrible lumps of dough were slightly less terrible than everyone else's today."

I put my hands on my hips and glared at him. "Zach. Are you trying to congratulate me? If not, scram."

"Scram? Scram? Have I stumbled into a gangster movie?"

I jabbed him in the kidney. Just then, Genna walked up to us. "Hello, Z."

"Hey, Matthews. Your friend here is trying to injure me."

"Maybe you should tell her what you did and she'll stop," Genna said. *Huh?*

"I doubt it," Zach replied.

"What are you talking about?" I demanded.

Zach looked at the ground and seemed to be edging away from us.

"He got you your blog followers at the last minute," Genna announced. "I couldn't think of anyone else we knew who wasn't at the Leaf the night before the deadline. So I checked the e-mail addresses of your last forty followers. Look."

She held up her phone and I peered at it. Sure enough, several of them had the name "Anderson" in the addresses.

Lots of them must've been employees of Zach's dad. A few of the names were familiar from school: Zach's friends.

"Wow," I said. "Thank you. I can't believe you did that."

"It wasn't a big deal," Zach said quietly. "And I wasn't spying on you either. I don't even know what's in a scone."

"I know." I sighed. "I'm sorry about that. It's just you were acting so weird after—"

Genna backed up then, mumbling something about needing more chai. I continued, "You know, after that thing in the storage room." Why couldn't I say the word "kiss"? It was like I was worried he didn't remember it and I would sound dumb.

"Yeah. I guess I was."

"So . . . are we friends, or what?" I really, really wanted to know.

"Friends? No, we're . . ." Zach kind of looked like he wanted to throw up. I smiled a little. A dash of Louisa's wisdom fluttered though my head, and I was certain of something just then. Zach did not want to be my boyfriend. Or anyone's boyfriend. Definitely not now. Maybe not ever.

". . . nemeses," I finished for him.

He immediately looked right at me then, more relieved than I'd ever seen him. "Exactly."

"You should get a haircut before school starts," I said. "Didn't anyone tell you faux hawks aren't cool anymore?"

"Ha! Didn't anyone tell you that a bright red creature of some sort is fighting with your head? And winning?"

"You should also buy some cologne or something. You still smell like algae," I added.

"You smell like . . . *ack!* You actually smell good. Can I get one of those?" I was still holding my award-winning toffee apple tea scones. I grinned.

He ate three of them, all the while telling me how awful they were.

Dear readers,

It's Annie again. Whew, what an exciting day. I thought I lost, but then it turned out I won! I'm so exhausted, but in a totally good way. I'm so pleased to share with you the winning recipe. I hope you like it.

Humbly yours always,
Annie Green

**Toffee Apple Tea Scones**

**Ingredients**
2 cups King Arthur all-purpose flour
1 tablespoon baking powder
⅓ cup sugar
½ teaspoon salt
Pinch of tea
3 tablespoons Lurpack butter
1 fresh egg
¾ cup fresh buttermilk
½ cup green apple, chopped
¼ cup English toffee pieces, chopped
   (I used Heath brand Bits o' Brickle toffee pieces)
¼ cup milk

For the glaze:
2 tablespoons brewed black tea, cooled
1 tablespoon butter
1 ½ cups confectioners' sugar (more to texture if necessary)
2 tablespoons whole milk
½ teaspoon vanilla extract

Preheat the oven to 400 degrees Fahrenheit. Mix the dry ingredients together first, then cut in the butter, toffee, apples, and egg. Slowly add the buttermilk to form a thick dough. Knead the dough on a board, roll to a 1-inch thickness, and cut the dough into 2-inch triangles. Place each triangle on a greased cookie sheet and brush the tops with milk. Bake for about 12 to 15 minutes in the oven until golden brown. While the scones are baking, brown the butter in a saucepan and add the brewed tea. Mix in the confectioners' sugar with a whisk. Add the milk until you have a thin glaze. Whisk in vanilla extract. Drizzle on top of the scones when they've cooled slightly; serve. Makes about 12 scones.

September 4  11:57 p.m.

## Chapter Twenty-Nine

When tea becomes ritual, it takes place at the heart
of our ability to see greatness in small things.
—MURIEL BARBERY, *THE ELEGANCE OF THE HEDGEHOG*

## Stuff I Have to Do the Day Before High School (High School . . . Aughhhhh!)

- Buy school supplies (notebooks, erasable pens, folders)
- Buy clothes (new jeans, a sweater, maybe some cute flats?)
- Get a HAIRCUT
- Drink calming tea
- Figure out where my homeroom is

- *Get some London guidebooks (okay, this doesn't have to happen today... but still)*
- *Have at least six spazzy IM conversations with Genna and Zoe*

Believe it or not, I accomplished all of that stuff. The lady at the salon used this thinning shears dealio on my hair and it looked amazing. Like a real hairstyle instead of a curl explosion. I knew that it would last precisely six hours, but I'd take it.

Genna and Zoe arrived at my front door the morning of our first day of school. I was so happy that the Teashop Girls had made plans to walk in together. Genna wore a bright lime green dress, striped leggings, and cute wedgies. Zoe was as crisp as ever in a white button-down shirt, white skirt, and fresh New Balance sneakers. She carried a navy blue sweater with her. I decided on jeans and a yellow blouse. I had a brand-new backpack and I actually felt ready. Over the summer I'd done everything I wanted to do. Now it was time for a new chapter.

"So, are you and Zach going to totally make out in front of your lockers?" Genna asked. It was seven a.m. I didn't even know where my locker *was*.

"Nope," I said. I smiled at Zoe, who rolled her eyes.

"Why not?" Genna wailed.

"It's just not like that, Gen. Sorry."

"Oh. Well, did I tell you guys I want to have a huge back-to-school party next weekend? We need to start making the food ahead of time because I want it to all be really good. And start trying to meet some upper-classmen right away because I don't want it to be all freshmen. . . ."

Zoe and I laughed. High school, we knew for sure, was going to be fun if Genna had anything to say about it.

"I can hardly even think about actual school," Zoe said then. "We're going to London!" Our trip would probably happen over winter break, because we all knew that Zo's parents wouldn't let her skip any school. I couldn't wait to begin planning it. I did manage to buy some guidebooks when I was supposed to be trying on school clothes the day before, and I was already compiling a mental list of spots I wanted to have tea at while we were there. Genna was making a list of the outfits she planned to take and the plays she wanted to see in the West End. Zoe wanted to do a side trip to the All England Lawn Tennis Club, where Wimbledon is held. We were all very excited. But before we conquered England, we needed to conquer high school. I knew we'd do it together, and that we would have an amazing four years. With tea whenever we needed it, of course. Suddenly the thought of high school didn't make me nervous at all. Not with Genna Matthews and Zoe Malik at my side. The original Teashop Girls could do anything.

We climbed the stairs to Madison West. Here we go!